The BIG Book of Ready-to-Go Writing Lessons

50 ENGAGING ACTIVITIES WITH GRAPHIC ORGANIZERS THAT TEACH
KIDS HOW TO TELL A STORY, CONVEY INFORMATION, DESCRIBE, PERSUADE, & MORE!

by Marcia Miller and Martin Lee

SCHOLASTIC
PROFESSIONALBOOKS

NEW YORK • TORONTO • LONDON • AUCKLAND • SYDNEY

MEXICO CITY • NEW DELHI • HONG KONG

Thanks, Matt

Cover design by Norma Ortiz
Cover and interior illustrations by Stephen Cox
Interior design by Grafica, Inc.

ISBN: 0-439-07747-8

Contents

PART 1: WRITE TO DESCRIBE

PART 2: WRITE TO NARRATE

PART 3: WRITE TO INFORM

PART 4: WRITE TO PERSUADE

PART 5: WRITE IN THE REAL WORLD

REPRODUCIBLES

Introduction

In *Writing: Teachers & Children at Work*, Donald H. Graves writes: "Children want to write . . . . Before they went to school they marked up walls, pavements, newspapers with crayons, chalk, pens or pencils . . . anything that makes a mark. The child's marks say, 'I am.'" As teachers, we want to guide students to write, and to help them take control of the writing process as a means to communicate in writing as freely, naturally, and effectively as they do when speaking. But good writing doesn't happen by magic.

What makes a good writer?

Answers to this question are as varied as writers themselves.

For children to become good writers, they have to write. And write more. They should experiment with fact and with fiction. They should experience different genres, styles, and purposes for writing. They should get their minds around varying degrees of complexity. They should wrestle with introductions, opinions, details, and conclusions. They need a purpose, an audience, and a platform. They need constructive feedback to help them improve their skills and see the power of their words. In so doing, young writers can gain the confidence to try again, and the courage to try new approaches and methods.

How can we help?

The craft of writing takes dreaming, thinking, and planning. A writer needs a goal and a sense of purpose. Yet most children are naturally inventive and creative, and they want to communicate. So, if we can provide them with the right kinds of stimulation, their writing will flow. Though all of our emerging authors may not become National Book Award candidates, we will have done our job if we can help them develop a sense of pleasure, confidence, and accomplishment as writers.

What does this book offer?

All writers and potential writers need a boost now and then. How many times have we heard student writers say, "I don't know what to write about!" "Where do I start?" "Is this enough?" or "How do I end this?" **The Big Book of Ready-To-Go Writing Lessons** attempts to address some of these concerns in meaningful, authentic, and enjoyable ways.

How to Use This Book ···································

This book presents 50 different writing ideas, presented in 5 parts:

Write to Describe
Write to Narrate
Write to Inform (Exposition)
Write to Persuade
Write in the Real World (Practical Writing)

Naturally, you'll find overlap within these categories. After all, it's pretty hard to persuade without describing or providing information. How good can a narrative be that leaves out rich description? Consult the table of contents. Each activity title is followed by a brief learning objective that summarizes the lesson's focus.

Each part opens with a brief statement of goals and techniques, and a list of evaluation tips for that kind of writing. Each part ends with more ideas for writing, which is a list of more than 20 additional "quickies" you might pursue. Develop them as you see fit.

Each lesson appears over two pages. The left-hand page is written to *you*. It provides clear and simple guidelines to help you facilitate the task. You need not do everything suggested. Pick and choose what works for you. All teacher pages have the same elements:

SET THE STAGE provides pre-writing ideas to engage students. It offers introductory matter, discussion questions, and one or more ideas you can consider to adapt the activity.

GUIDE THE WAY gives suggestions for ways to help students move through the

task. These may point out likely responses, highlight common stumbling blocks, or present tips to help students achieve better results. This part always ends with an item to be read directly to students. This is a tip that focuses on a pertinent aspect of the writing process, the genre, or the writing mode. You might post these on chart paper.

FOLLOW IT UP gives a few ideas for presenting, publishing, or extending the activities.

The right-hand page is a reproducible for *students*, and begins with the directive **WRITE AWAY!** These pages vary from task to task. They provide different kinds of structure and guidance. Some are graphic organizers. Others are checklists of points to consider. Others are templates students may fill in. You'll find formats that help students formulate and organize their ideas and find their own voices. All student pages have the same elements:

This symbol highlights a definition, key idea, or fundamental concept for the task.

This pencil means, "Write!" Sometimes students will write directly onto the page. Other times, they will use their own paper.

And NOW— This section is a way to wrap up the task. It might have students use their notes to create first drafts. It might offer ideas for revising or presenting; it might give one last writer's tip they can apply.

Teacher Tips

★ Move through the book as you see fit. Do activities in any order that makes sense for your class or schedule.

★ You may find that some activities are too advanced for your class, while others may be too basic. Some may take more time than you have. Others may take less time than you planned. Feel free to revise or extend tasks to suit your students' needs.

★ Use the writing tasks in this book as full lessons, warm-ups, homework assignments, writing corner activities, group projects, or performance assessments.

★ Determine the best grouping to suit your teaching style, and the learning styles and levels of independence of your students. Invite them to work individually, in pairs, in small groups, or as an entire class.

★ Encourage sharing, discussing, analyzing, and summarizing of students' writing. Establish an atmosphere that promotes intellectual exploration and an appreciation and respect for each other as writers, thinkers, and problem-solvers. Help make children feel comfortable as writers so they'll begin to choose to write on their own, without external prompts or assignments.

★ For whole class activities copy the graphic organizers on to the chart paper in enlarged versions. You might also suggest that students copy the graphic organizers on separate sheets of paper.

★ Use the reproducibles at the end of the book. There you will find a Self-Evaluation Checklist, a helpful list of editor's marks, and four different certificates of encouragement you can present to young writers as circumstances dictate.

★ Take advantage of any writing opportunities that present themselves on any given day. Talk about them, work out a pre-writing plan, or model a final product—whichever suits the task.

★ Set up a writing center in your classroom. There, you can place some of these activities for students to do on their own, or you can present examples of completed works and works-in-progress. Provide a variety of writing supplies, story starters, dictionaries, thesauruses, inspiring quotations, author biographies, and so on.

★ Be a role model. Show that you, too, are a working writer who must think about, plan, try out, fix, and polish your own work until you are satisfied with it.

★ Involve parents. Present some of these writing ideas at parent meetings or conferences to highlight the value of this component in your language arts program.

Write to Describe

The goal of **descriptive** writing is to describe in written terms a person, a place, a thing, or an idea. Descriptive writing expresses and develops images through the use of precise sensory words and phrases. Descriptive writing should enable readers to smell, taste, hear, touch, and see what the subject is like.

Techniques of descriptive writing include figurative language such as simile and metaphor; sound devices such as alliteration, rhyme, and assonance; and sensory imagery.

EVALUATION TIPS

There are many ways to evaluate students' descriptive writing. Here are some broad points to consider as you judge some or all of the writing activities in this section of the book:

Does the descriptive piece have—

- ❑ A stated purpose or clear focus?
- ❑ A plan of organization?
- ❑ A variety of sensory details?
- ❑ Vivid images?
- ❑ A unique slant?

- ❑ Is the piece complete?
- ❑ Does it allow readers to visualize a person, place, or event?
- ❑ Does it show planning and follow-through?
- ❑ Is the word choice thoughtful, precise, and descriptive?
- ❑ How are the mechanics (grammar, usage, spelling, punctuation)?

Ideal Hideaway

Students will describe places they wish they could escape to, to be by themselves.

SET THE STAGE

★ Read a poem about hideaways such as "Hold Fast Your Dreams" by Louise Driscoll.

★ Display pictures of retreats, such as clubhouses, trees, dens, the Bat Cave, and so on.

★ Discuss questions like these: *Have you ever wanted to disappear into a special secret place that only YOU know about? What would that place look like? Where would it be? How big would it be? When would you go there? Who else would be allowed in?*

★ Duplicate and distribute the idea organizer on page 11, which students can use to help them collect their thoughts and ideas.

★ Suggest that students imagine adapting existing spaces in their own homes.

GUIDE THE WAY

★ Have students think about the physical attributes of the hideaway including appearance, size, location, view, shape, furnishing, access, and so on.

★ Help kids add *pizzazz*! Descriptive words can help writers make hideaways seem all the more unique and valued. Provide a thesaurus, or present new words kids can include. Words like *haven, sanctuary,* or *retreat* are more evocative than *place* or *spot*.

★ Invite writers to describe the feelings or sensations they get when they are safe within their hideaways.

> **Tone**—*Does your description make the hideaway sound really special to you?*

FOLLOW IT UP

★ Have students accompany their writing with sketches or diagrams of the hideaways.

★ Place each completed piece in an envelope. Put the envelopes in a shoebox "hideaway" stapled to a bulletin board. Invite each student to pick an envelope and read about a different hideaway, then return the piece to the shoebox for others to enjoy.

★ Extend by having students write about times when they would have gone to their hideaways.

Name: _____

WRITE AWAY!
Ideal Hideaway

🔑 To write about a place, first think about things that make it special.

✏️ Jot down ideas to use later when you draft your piece.

⭐ Reasons for having a hideaway: _____

_____

_____

⭐ Places to set up your hideaway: _____

_____

_____

⭐ Who would know about it? _____

_____

⭐ Who would NOT know about it? _____

_____

⭐ Comforting objects for your hideaway: _____

_____

_____

⭐ Others words for—

ideal	hideaway	safe
	.	

And NOW—

Use the ideas and words you gathered to write a description of your ideal hideaway. Remember—your hideaway is the only one of its kind. Make it sound perfect—for you.

Catchy Captions

Students will write captivating captions—brief and punchy descriptions of events or images.

Jo and Liz hang on tight.

⭐ SET THE STAGE

★ Define *caption* as a short description given below a cartoon, drawing, or photograph.

★ Display an assortment of captioned images from newspapers, magazines, yearbooks, catalogs, or other sources.

★ Discuss questions like these: *Why are captions short? What kinds of details do captions include? How can a caption improve someone's appreciation of an image?*

★ Provide an assortment of pictures, photos, or cartoons. Have students select one (or more) at random, or by preference, about which to write a catchy caption.

★ You might establish a length limit, such as 3 sentences, 50 words, or 4 lines.

★ Duplicate and distribute the writer's framework on page 13.

★ Students might draw original pictures for which to write captions. Suggest vivid situations they can visualize, such as a daredevil stunt, a riotous circus act, a thrilling amusement park ride, a once-in-a-lifetime moment, or a family reunion.

⭐ GUIDE THE WAY

★ By definition, captions are brief, but they need not be dull. Help students focus their descriptive captions by replacing commonplace words with sparkling substitutes. For example, why say funny if you can say "goofy" or "hilarious?"

> **Add!**—*Captions should take up where the visuals leave off. Enhance an image by adding description, not just by restating the obvious. Create captions that make readers want to know more.*

⭐ FOLLOW IT UP

★ Create an interactive bulletin board with two parts. On one side, present the visuals; on the other side, present the captions. Can students match them up?

★ Challenge students to create new and improved captions for images found in classroom books. For instance, they can make captions more interesting, wittier, more richly detailed, more factual, or more reader-friendly.

Name: _____

Jo and Liz hang on tight.

WRITE AWAY!
Catchy Captions

 A *caption* describes details of a picture. A good caption is short and to the point. It adds words for what the picture can't show. It makes readers want to know more.

Put a picture, drawing, photo, graph, or cartoon below. Look at it carefully. Then create a catchy caption for it. What descriptions will bring the image to life?

_____

_____

_____

_____

_____

And NOW—

Reread your caption. Does it grab the readers' interest? Does it help them better understand the image? Does it make them want to know more? Does it read smoothly?

Name That Character!

Students will depict characters by creating descriptive names for them and by writing brief character sketches that support the names.

Cranky the Clown

SET THE STAGE

★ Brainstorm with students to list descriptive names, nicknames, or aliases for real or fictional characters. Focus on ones that describe, such as Cruella DeVil (from *101 Dalmatians*), the Wicked Witch of the West (from *The Wizard of Oz*), Honest Abe (Lincoln), or Michael "Air" Jordan.

★ Discuss questions like these: *What can a name or nickname describe about someone? What attributes or qualities might nicknames feature? Can a nickname describe more than one trait? How can a name or nickname affect how you feel about a character?*

★ Have each student pick a person or character. Ask students to first jot down key traits of the people or characters, then create nicknames for them. Finally, tell them to write a paragraph that describes the character and tells why the nickname fits.

★ Duplicate and distribute the character web on page 15.

★ Vary the task by having students create new names or nicknames for themselves. The name can offer a descriptive peek into personality, talents, skills, or habits.

★ Invite students to create original characters to name, nickname, and describe.

GUIDE THE WAY

★ Good descriptions show, not just tell. It's okay to say that a person is clever; it's far better to provide an example of his or her cleverness.

★ Urge writers to describe actions, words, features, and traits, and not to just give opinions.

Alive!—*Descriptions should bring characters to life, as if you truly know them.*

FOLLOW IT UP

★ Display the descriptions and names in a "Character Gallery."

★ Extend the activity by having students create acronym poems from the characters' names. Each letter in a name begins a line of the poem. The finished poem should present an overall description of the person.

Name: _____

★ WRITE AWAY!
Name That Character!

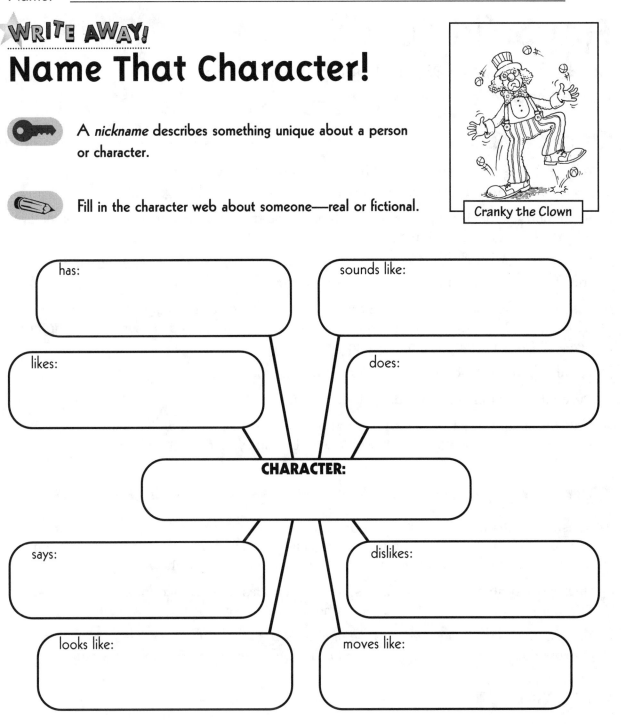

🔑 A *nickname* describes something unique about a person or character.

✏️ Fill in the character web about someone—real or fictional.

Cranky the Clown

| has: | sounds like: |

| likes: | does: |

CHARACTER:

| says: | dislikes: |

| looks like: | moves like: |

And NOW—

Study your web. Create a descriptive name or nickname that fits your subject. Then write a brief character sketch. Be sure to support the name or nickname with lively details.

Flavorful Foods

Students will write descriptions of favorite food
items that address all five senses.

SET THE STAGE

★ Play the song "Food, Glorious Food" from the musical *Oliver!* Or show an eating scene
from a movie to whet students' appetites for this writing task.

★ Read aloud some descriptions of delectable foods from restaurant reviews, cookbooks,
advertisements, or health magazines.

★ Review the five senses—sight, taste, touch, smell, and sound—and talk about some of
the ways that foods engage each of these senses.

★ Discuss questions like these: *What helps you decide what foods you like? What kinds of
details fit a description of food? What kinds of words can you use to discuss the different
senses? How much description is enough?*

★ Duplicate and distribute the sensory details chart on page 17.

★ Students might prefer to try describing fancy foods for pets!

★ Students might describe foods for a particular audience, such as fussy toddlers, gour-
met adults, junk-food lovers, or people who like spicy foods.

GUIDE THE WAY

★ Sensory details make food descriptions all the more delectable. Remind students to
consider not just how the food tastes, smells, and feels, but also its color and texture,
and the sounds it makes when they slice, peel, open, bite, or chew it.

★ Suggest that students use modifiers, such as similes, to enhance their descriptions.
For instance, a bowl of chili that is "as hot as a tin roof in August" is really spicy!

Be Precise—*Have you used a range of clear, strong sensory details? It's easy to say
that pudding is tasty. It's more descriptive to call it* velvety, golden brown, *or* lumpy.

FOLLOW IT UP

★ Create a fantasy menu of fabulous foods that students have described.

★ Have a "tasting" where students sample new foods, preferably uncommon ones.
Encourage them to respond to the foods by writing descriptions based on
their perceptions.

★ Compile a class cookbook of family recipes with descriptions students write.

Name: _____

Flavorful Foods

 For everything we eat, we use some—or all—of our five senses.

 Pick a food that you love. Use your five senses to describe it.

The food: _____

How it LOOKS	
How it FEELS	
How it SMELLS	
How it SOUNDS	
How it TASTES	

And NOW—

Use the sensory details to write a delicious description of the dish. Describe the food so well that mouths water, eyes roll, and stomachs growl!

Blockbuster Blurbs

Students will create capsule summaries of books or movies to attract an audience.

Great Holiday Reading!

SET THE STAGE

★ Define *blurb* as a short piece written about a product in order to interest people in it. Students have probably read blurbs on video boxes or book covers. Help them think of a blurb as a kind of brief book report or film review, such as they might read in the TV listings of the newspaper. Better blurbs may attract bigger audiences.

★ Have students read blurbs from the card catalog, movie review books, or travel guides.

★ Focus on how to write effective blurbs by discussing questions like these: *What details attract you to a book or movie? What should not go in a blurb? Do you think a blurb can make someone not want to see a film or read a book? Should a blurb give opinions?*

★ Duplicate and distribute the purpose profile on page 19. Be sure students understand the purpose of each category in the profile so they can complete it effectively.

★ You may want to provide a list of book or movie titles from which students choose. Students who select the same subject can compare blurbs.

★ Vary by having students write blurbs for something other than books or movies. They might write about products, games, pieces of sports gear, performances, or vacation destinations.

GUIDE THE WAY

★ Help writers identify their purposes or goals and the audience they wish to attract.

★ Blurbs, by definition, try to draw interest. Guide writers to use descriptive words and phrases to make their subjects sound exciting, inviting, and too good to miss!

★ Enthusiasm can enliven a blurb. Help writers pick subjects they would be glad to recommend.

Caution—Don't spill the beans! A blurb should never reveal so much that it spoils the experience for others.

FOLLOW IT UP

★ Have students rewrite existing blurbs for books they've read or films they've seen.

★ Ask the school librarian to explain where the blurbs come from that appear on catalog cards. Students might offer to augment existing cards.

★ Publish book blurbs in a class literary newsletter so classmates can get ideas before they go to the library. Similarly, publish movie blurbs in a class film guide.

Name: _____

WRITE AWAY!
Blockbuster Blurbs

Great Holiday Reading!

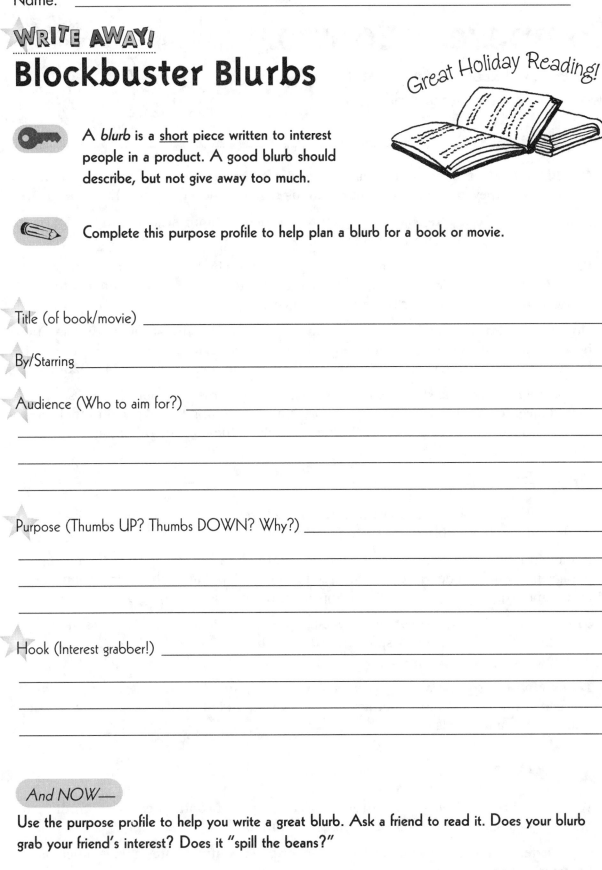

🔑 A *blurb* is a <u>short</u> piece written to interest people in a product. A good blurb should describe, but not give away too much.

✏️ Complete this purpose profile to help plan a blurb for a book or movie.

⭐ Title (of book/movie) _____

⭐ By/Starring _____

⭐ Audience (Who to aim for?) _____

_____

_____

_____

⭐ Purpose (Thumbs UP? Thumbs DOWN? Why?) _____

_____

_____

_____

⭐ Hook (Interest grabber!) _____

_____

_____

_____

And NOW—

Use the purpose profile to help you write a great blurb. Ask a friend to read it. Does your blurb grab your friend's interest? Does it "spill the beans?"

Compare & Contrast

Students will describe the ways in which two items are similar and different.

SET THE STAGE

★ Clarify the distinction between *comparing* and *contrasting*: We *compare* items when we describe how they are alike. We *contrast* items when we describe how they differ.

★ Display pairs of concrete objects (or pictures of them) to spur students to think about ways to compare and contrast them.

★ Share *All Kinds of Feet* by Ron and Nancy Goor, *Heads* by Ron and Nancy Goor, and/or *Breathtaking Noses* by Hana Machotka. Use these books to stimulate students to notice and discuss similarities and differences.

★ Duplicate and distribute the Venn diagram on page 21. Be sure students understand how this diagram is used to organize details on two subjects. They may be interested to know that the tool is named for English mathematician John Venn (1834–1923).

★ Challenge more advanced students to compare and contrast two objects that seem, at first glance, totally unrelated, such as a brick and a bowling ball. Appeal to their creativity and cleverness to detect similarities as well as the obvious differences.

GUIDE THE WAY

★ You might make a set of cards with words or pictures on them. Students pick any two cards and use those objects for their description.

★ Demonstrate how the Venn diagram can be a paragraph organizer. To write a compare paragraph, students describe the features in the overlapping region. For a contrast paragraph, they describe details that appear in the two separate regions.

> **Order**—*Think about how to organize a compare and contrast piece. There are many ways to do this. One way is first to identify both objects. Then describe all the ways in which they are alike, followed by a description of how they differ.*
>
> **Transitions**—*Use words that guide the way in comparisons and contrasts. Think about words and phrases like* on the other hand, however, *and* although; *or* similarly, by the same token, *and* likewise.

FOLLOW IT UP

★ You might direct students to organize their compare and contrast essays according to different plans, such as a point-by-point presentation.

★ As an extension, suggest that students compare and contrast three things, such as a hamster, a gerbil, and a guinea pig, using a 3-circle Venn diagram.

Name: _____

★ WRITE AWAY!
Compare & Contrast

🔑 A *Venn diagram* is a tool to organize ideas about how things are alike and different. It can show, at a glance, details you can use to compare and contrast.

✏️ Pick two objects: _____
In the top circle, list details that are true only for one object.
In the bottom circle, list details that are true only for the other object.
Where the circles overlap, list details that are true for *both*.

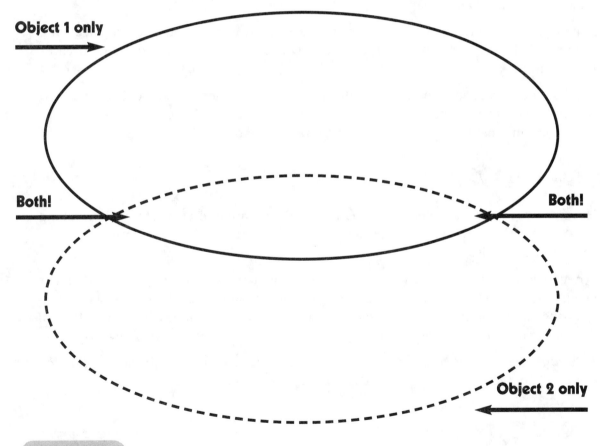

Object 1 only

Both!

Both!

Object 2 only

And NOW—

Use the details to write a description that compares and contrasts the objects. First, identify them. Next, tell how they are alike. Then, tell how they are different. Remember to use transition words and phrases for smooth reading.

Sweet Dreams

Students will describe dreams they have had—or wish they had!

SET THE STAGE

★ Turn down the lights and ask students to think back on dreams they have had that stick in their minds. It might be a happy dream, an odd dream, a scary dream, or a daydream.

★ Play the poignant song "Castle on a Cloud" (from *Les Misérables*). In it, young Cosette sings of a place she dreams about where she is always happy.

★ Discuss questions like these: *What makes you remember a dream? Why does the memory of some dreams last a long time, while others fade quickly? What details help make a dream unforgettable?*

★ Duplicate and distribute the dreamscape diagram on page 23. As the dream "floats," students follow "thought bubbles" to clouds where they jot down details the dream may include.

★ A dream doesn't always make sense. It may not be in order. These qualities make dreams an excellent topic for free-writing. You may want to have students free-write about dreams instead of, or in addition to, using the dreamscape diagram.

GUIDE THE WAY

★ Have pairs of students retell their dreams (or daydreams) to each other. By retelling dreams and then answering a partners' questions, students may be better able to recall more details.

★ When students are ready to write about their dreams, remind them to include lots of sensory details. One of the fabulous things about dreams is that they can be full of amazing sights, sounds, smells, tastes, and sensations of touch. Encourage them also to include descriptions of how they felt both in the dreams and after they woke up.

> *Privacy*—You may have trouble recalling a dream. Or you may prefer not to share a real dream. If so, feel free to describe a daydream or a wish instead.

FOLLOW IT UP

★ Collect dream descriptions in a binder, or post them in cloudbursts on a bulletin board.

★ Have students read dream descriptions onto audio tape. Let students listen to the tape during free time, or play parts of it to help them wind down at the end of class.

★ Extend by having students interview friends or family members to hear about dreams they have had. Students can write descriptions of these dreams to add to the class collection.

Name: _____

WRITE AWAY!
Sweet Dreams

🔑 Dreams can be jumbled and confusing. They can be sweet, beautiful, or weird! But they usually have lots of details you can describe.

✏️ Fill in the dreamscape diagram. Then follow the bubbles of "thought" as your dream floats along. Write details inside the clouds attached to the threads of thoughts.

And NOW—

Use your dreamscape diagram to help you write a full description of your dream. Don't forget to write a title. Use lots of rich details. Describe how you felt—during the dream and after you woke up.

In Animal Territory

Students will write descriptions of animals' behavior.

SET THE STAGE

★ Put a variety of classroom animals on display. If you don't have a class menagerie, you might temporarily borrow some from other classrooms, or have volunteers bring in "portable pets" from home. Possibilities include fish, mice, gerbils, hamsters, frogs, turtles, hermit crabs, meal worms, lizards, ants (in see-through "farms"), or parakeets.

★ Tell students that scientists observe animals in their natural habitats so they can learn about their life cycles, movements, ways of communicating and interacting, and diet.

★ Read students a passage from *Never Cry Wolf* by Farley Mowatt, which includes vivid observations of arctic wolves in the wild.

★ Duplicate and distribute the observation log on page 25. Tell students that they will use it for taking notes during their observations.

★ Assign this activity for students to do at home. They can observe pets, birds that visit their backyard feeder, or neighborhood animals (domestic or wild). Emphasize that students should exercise extreme caution with animals or pets they don't know. They should infer how these unknown animals or pets might smell or feel.

★ If live animals are unavailable for observation, show a nature video without the sound. That way, students can focus on what they observe, not on the narration.

GUIDE THE WAY

★ To help focus students' observations, suggest that they notice how the animals eat, drink, play, sleep, sound, move, clean themselves, or interact with other animals or humans during the observation period.

★ Set up observation posts near the classroom animals, where students can sit and observe, take notes, and record details. You might provide hand lenses to help students get a closer look at some of the animals' characteristics or activities.

Action!—*You can make descriptions more exciting with action verbs that are vivid and precise.* The hamster scrambled onto the wheel *paints a livelier image than* The hamster got on the wheel.

FOLLOW IT UP

★ Have students who observed the same animals share their observations in groups.

★ Plan an observation field trip to a zoo, a bird sanctuary, an aquarium, a kennel, an animal shelter, or another place where students can observe live animals.

Name: _____

In Animal Territory

 An *observation* describes what you witness over time. Record details as they occur. Pick an animal to observe for 5 minutes. Focus on the creature the whole time.

Record what you see, hear, smell, and touch (be very careful!). Notice the animal's physical features, how it moves, and what it does. Use lots of details!

⭐ The animal: _____

⭐ Its habitat: _____

⭐ Time of observation: _____

How it **looks**	
How it **sounds**	
How it **smells**	
How it **feels**	
How it **moves**	
What it **does**	

And NOW—

Use the details above to write a description of the animal's behavior during the time you observed it.

New Point of View

Students will write descriptions from
the viewpoint of inanimate objects.

SET THE STAGE

★ Explain that *point of view* refers to who tells a story. "First-person" point of view means that a character in the story tells it. First-person stories use *I*, *me*, and *mine*.

★ Read an excerpt from a story told in the first person such as *My Side of the Mountain* by Jean Craighead George or *Ben and Me* by Robert Lawson.

★ You might also read the poem "Point of View" by Shel Silverstein (from *Where the Sidewalk Ends*).

★ Define the word *inanimate* as "not alive or non-living." Brainstorm with students to list inanimate objects in the classroom, such as books, shoes, desks, backpacks, or water.

★ Have each student pick an inanimate object, and write a descriptive piece told from its point of view. Discuss questions like these: *What object will you be? What problems or concerns would you face? How would the world look from your new point of view? What misunderstandings might you now face? What feelings could you now have?*

★ Duplicate, distribute, and discuss the W's organizer on page 27. As students answer these questions, they will create the details they can use in their descriptive pieces.

★ You might have student pairs brainstorm ideas for this task before they write.

GUIDE THE WAY

★ Provide ample thinking time.

★ Spark students' creativity by helping them imagine how to personify objects. For example, would a pen complain about standing on its nose to write? Would a boot complain about trudging through mud and snow? Might an envelope hurt when you tear it open? Would water in an ice-cube tray shiver when it goes in the freezer?

Take Charge—In real life, inanimate objects have no thoughts or feelings. But if you are a creative writer, you can give an object intelligence, pride, anger, a sense of humor, or any other trait, feeling, or attitude. Be clever, outrageous, or funny!

FOLLOW IT UP

★ Have students share their descriptive pieces with classmates.

★ Publish the pieces in an "Inanimate Anthology."

Name: _____

New Point of View

🔑 Suppose an object could tell its own story. What might it say? What might it complain about? What might it long for? What might it love?

✏️ Pick an object. Become that object! Imagine events in its life. Answer the W's to help create a story about the object.

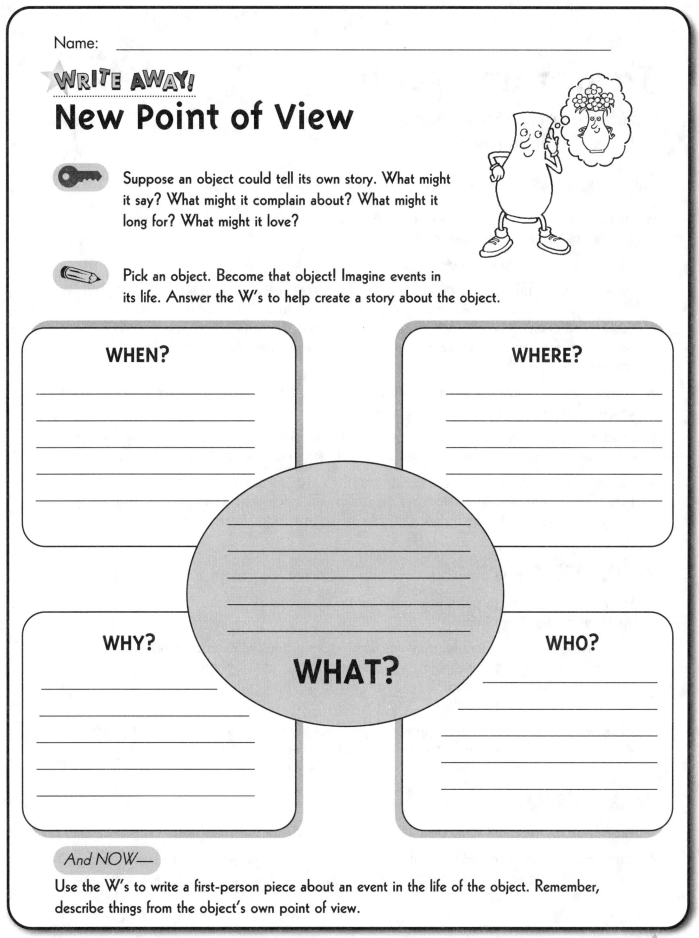

WHEN?
_____
_____
_____
_____
_____

WHERE?
_____
_____
_____
_____
_____

WHAT?
_____
_____
_____
_____
_____

WHY?
_____
_____
_____
_____

WHO?
_____
_____
_____
_____

And NOW—

Use the W's to write a first-person piece about an event in the life of the object. Remember, describe things from the object's own point of view.

Target on Sports

Students will describe sporting events or other kinds of contests.

SET THE STAGE

★ Display an assortment of sports-related pictures, equipment, souvenirs, trading cards, magazines, uniforms, and so on.

★ Play excerpts from a video tape of sports highlights.

★ Pose questions like these: *If you were describing a sports event, what details would you include? What descriptions would you give? What would you leave out? How can you build excitement? Who or what would you describe: The fans? The players? The playing field? The coaches, mascots, referees, or cheerleaders? Should you describe all participants or focus on one or two?*

★ Duplicate and distribute the sports target on page 29. Students can use this organizer to gather details for their descriptive pieces.

★ Students who have little acquaintance with or interest in sports might focus instead on other kinds of contests, such as spelling bees, sing-downs, or chess matches.

★ As alternatives, students might create trading cards for imaginary players, with a picture on one side, and statistics and details on the back that describe the athlete's accomplishments. Or they might describe new team logos or mascots.

GUIDE THE WAY

★ Have students work in pairs or groups to discuss sensory details associated with the sporting events they choose.

★ After students gather details, they will write descriptions of exciting moments in the sports events—the winning point, a fantastic fielding feat, a photo-finish, and so on. Encourage students to make the moments thrilling and engaging enough to have them broadcast on sports radio or TV.

> *Point of View*—*Will you write from the point of view of an athlete? A fan? A coach? A groundskeeper? A trainer? An official or judge? A winner? A loser?*

FOLLOW IT UP

★ Have students present their descriptions in a mock sports broadcast.

★ Challenge students to watch actual sports events and then write about the events as if they were giving the play-by-play commentary, or covering the events for a newspaper.

Name: _____

Target on Sports

 Sports, like most activities, have lots of details to describe.

 Pick a sporting event. List the people who take part. Describe the location. Then fill in details about sights, sounds, feelings, smells, and tastes that fit the event.

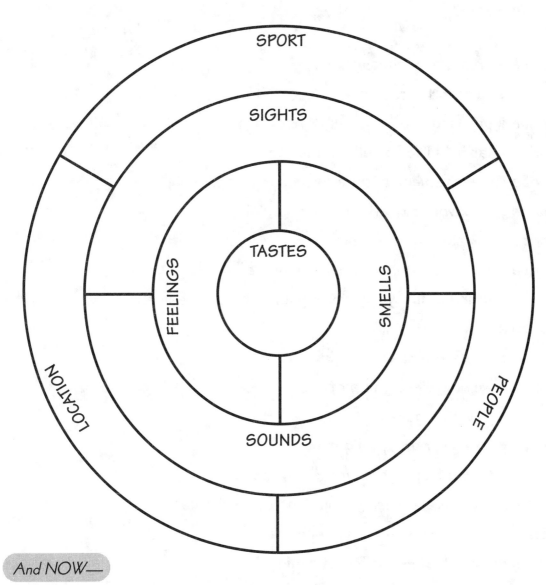

SPORT

SIGHTS

TASTES

FEELINGS

SMELLS

LOCATION

PEOPLE

SOUNDS

And NOW—

Use the ideas in the target to write a description of a key moment in the event.
Make the description exciting and dramatic. Make the moment come alive.

More Ideas for Descriptive Writing

- ❑ Describe waking up.
- ❑ Describe your earliest memory.
- ❑ Describe your kindergarten teacher.
- ❑ Describe learning something important.
- ❑ Describe an event that occurs in nature.
- ❑ Describe a puppet.
- ❑ Describe a dinosaur.
- ❑ Describe an old family photograph.
- ❑ Describe your favorite costume.
- ❑ Describe a painting.
- ❑ Describe what it is like to build something.
- ❑ Describe the excitement of an awards ceremony.
- ❑ Describe your favorite television commercial.
- ❑ Describe being caught in a storm.
- ❑ Describe sleeping outdoors under the stars.
- ❑ Describe opening a dusty old box in your attic or basement.
- ❑ Describe a brave deed.
- ❑ Describe sounds you hear at night.
- ❑ Describe a window display in a store.
- ❑ Describe a clever disguise.
- ❑ Describe packing for an overnight trip.
- ❑ Describe how you feel on the last day of school.
- ❑ Describe what you see when you look at puffy clouds.
- ❑ Describe an amazing sight you've seen.
- ❑ Describe getting lost—and found again.

Write to Narrate

The goal of **narrative** writing is to tell stories. Narrative writing works best when it presents and develops a story in an organized manner. Narrative writing should carry readers along and make them want to know what will happen next.

Narrative writing techniques focus on the effective use of basic story elements—a setting in time and place, central characters, a plot, a conflict, and a resolution. Narrative writing needs a beginning, a middle, and an end, and many vivid details that bring the tale to life.

EVALUATION TIPS

There are many ways to evaluate students' narrative writing. Here are some broad points to consider as you judge some or all of the writing activities in this section of the book:

Does the narrative piece have—

- ❑ A clear beginning, middle, and end?
- ❑ A way to engage readers from the start?
- ❑ Specific characters, setting, and plot?
- ❑ Vivid details?
- ❑ Realistic dialogue (if applicable)?
- ❑ A consistent point of view?
- ❑ Transitions and indications of order?

- ❑ Is the piece complete?
- ❑ Does it allow readers to follow a story?
- ❑ Does it reach its intended audience?
- ❑ Does it show planning and follow-through?
- ❑ Is the word choice thoughtful, precise, and descriptive?
- ❑ How are the mechanics (grammar, usage, spelling, punctuation)?

Amusing Anecdote

Students will write brief stories that tell about something that once happened to them.

⭐ SET THE STAGE

★ Define an *anecdote* as a short, often funny story about a real-life event. Anecdotes are brief remembrances, usually written in an informal way. An anecdote focuses on the event itself, and what the writer learned from it.

★ Read some anecdotes to students, or provide copies for them to read independently. Ask the librarian to help you find examples in anthologies, magazines, or texts.

★ Discuss questions like these: *What odd or amusing thing has happened to you lately that you want to tell others? What part(s) of the event is most interesting to share? What is unnecessary to include? How can you make an anecdote interesting to others?*

★ Duplicate and distribute the chain of events organizer on page 33. Be sure students understand how to use this tool to organize the sequence of events for the anecdote.

★ Anecdotes work well when presented orally. You might have students use the chain of events organizers to plan their anecdotes. Then they can share the anecdotes aloud in small groups, on tape, or before the whole class.

⭐ GUIDE THE WAY

★ Have students work in pairs or small groups to talk through their anecdotes. By telling stories aloud, students can gain insight into how to write them effectively.

★ Like any narrative, an anecdote needs a beginning, a middle, and an end. Encourage peer-to-peer feedback so writers can make their anecdotes more clear and complete.

> **Humor**—*In an anecdote, humor is best when it pokes fun at the person who tells the tale—you! Make the humor gentle, not mocking. Will your anecdote make an audience smile or laugh? Behind the humor, what do you reveal about yourself?*

⭐ FOLLOW IT UP

★ Have students collect amusing anecdotes in a binder you might entitle, "Did You Hear About the Time When I . . .?"

★ Ask students to write anecdotes about an event they all experienced. This strategy can highlight how each person has a slightly different take on the same situation.

Name: _____

Amusing Anecdote

 An *anecdote* is a brief, often funny story about something that really happened to you.

 Gather details in this chain for an anecdote about the time you _____

_____.

First, _____
_____
_____

Next, _____
_____
_____
_____

Then, _____
_____
_____

Finally,
_____
_____
_____
_____
_____
_____

What I learned: _____
_____
_____
_____

And NOW—

Use the details to write your anecdote. Keep it brief, but clear. Read it aloud to check that the details are in order. Is the message clear? Does the humor come through?

Dear Diary

Students will write diary entries that narrate real or fictional experiences.

SET THE STAGE

★ Brainstorm with students about why people keep diaries or journals.

★ Read an excerpt from a diary, such as *A Diary From Dixie* by Mary Chesnut; from a work that contains diary entries, such as *Harriet the Spy* by Louise Fitzhugh or *Ashleigh's Diary* by Joanna Campbell, or from *A Book of Your Own: Keeping a Diary or Journal* by Carla Stevens.

★ Discuss questions like these: *In what ways is writing in a diary different from writing other narratives? When is a good time to write in a diary? How can keeping a diary help you "unwind" or think back on things that have happened?*

★ Duplicate and distribute the diary details sheet on page 35.

★ Pairs of students might want to write dialogue diaries. In this kind of diary, each person writes to the other about experiences or ideas, knowing that the entry is meant to be shared. Students then exchange diaries and write their responses to each other. Thus, a dialogue diary is like a conversation that takes place in writing.

GUIDE THE WAY

★ To get students started you might suggest that they list interesting things they have heard or seen, or the names of noteworthy people. Or, have them jot down phrases or words they like. Some might reflect on a historical event and imagine that they were there.

★ Encourage students to write freely, to explore thoughts, feelings, opinions, or ideas.

Archive—*Date your diary entry. Indicate where you were when you wrote it, and add any other details that can describe the time or place. That way, when you go back to read the diary entry later on, you'll recall the setting.*

FOLLOW IT UP

★ Have students actually keep diaries for a period of time, such as a week or a month. Encourage them to write in their diaries regularly.

★ Challenge students to create diary entries written from the viewpoints of pets.

Name: _____

WRITE AWAY!
Dear Diary

 A diary is a personal record of events. Be a *diarist*—somebody who keeps a diary.

✏️ Some people write in their diaries every day. Others only write in them from time to time. Here are some guidelines to help you get organized:

⭐ What's your favorite writing tool? [You can be picky!] _____

⭐ Where is your favorite writing place or writing position? [Ernest Hemingway, a famous American writer, wrote standing up!] _____

_____

⭐ When's the best time for you to write? [Early? Late? Before/after something?] _____

_____

⭐ Would you let others read your diary? Who? _____

_____

⭐ Now, think of questions to ponder, such as:

- Why is that?
- What bothers me?
- Who matters to me?
- How do I feel about _____?
- What made this day great?
- Where will I be ten years from now?
- What do I want to remember forever?

(And NOW—)

Write a diary entry. Begin with "Dear Diary." Write to the diary like it's a friend. Be informal and chatty. Or be serious. Or be funny. Just be yourself!

A Dark and Stormy Night

Students will write scary stories they might share at sleepovers.

SET THE STAGE

★ Display pictures or other art that suggest fear or suspense.

★ Turn down the lights and pull down the shades. Read a scary poem, play evocative music (like "In the Hall of the Mountain King" from *Peer Gynt* by Edvard Grieg), or sing creepy songs.

★ Discuss questions like these: *Why do people like to tell and hear scary stories? What makes a story scary? How can you use words to create frightening feelings?*

★ Duplicate and distribute the scare guide on page 37. Discuss how students can use it to collect narrative details for their stories, such as scary sounds, scary sights, scary scenes, and scary words to enhance their tales.

★ Students might work in groups to collaborate on scary stories. They can brainstorm together to create characters, settings, and situations that fill the spine-chilling bill.

★ To stimulate scary creativity, hold a storytelling session in which students share scary stories they have heard, read, or seen in movies or on television. Or invite a professional storyteller or folklorist to the class to set the scene.

GUIDE THE WAY

★ Remind students that stories need not be gory or gruesome to be scary.

★ Discuss narrative elements writers can use to build scariness, such as weird characters, strange settings, unexpected plot twists, or unexplained developments. Remind writers that, like any other kind of story, a scary story has a beginning, a middle, and an end.

★ Encourage the use of vivid verbs, such as *howl*, *menace*, or *tremble*, and electrifying adjectives, such as *spine-tingling*, *sinister*, or *ruthless*. Supply a thesaurus and dictionary.

> **Suspense**—*Don't just frighten your audience with a big loud BOO! Great scary stories build suspense over time. They may reveal, bit by bit, a terrible secret. They may slowly introduce a strange character. They may exaggerate every day sounds and sights to make them seem creepy. Build suspense slowly up to the most thrilling and terrifying moments!*

FOLLOW IT UP

★ Have students read aloud their scary stories.

★ Help students tape-record their stories, along with sound effects, if possible. Let them borrow the tapes so they can share their stories with friends and families.

Name: _____

A Dark and Stormy Night

🔑 Scary stories stir up feelings of fear. Luckily, they are just stories!

✏️ Plan a scary story by listing creepy details in this scare guide!

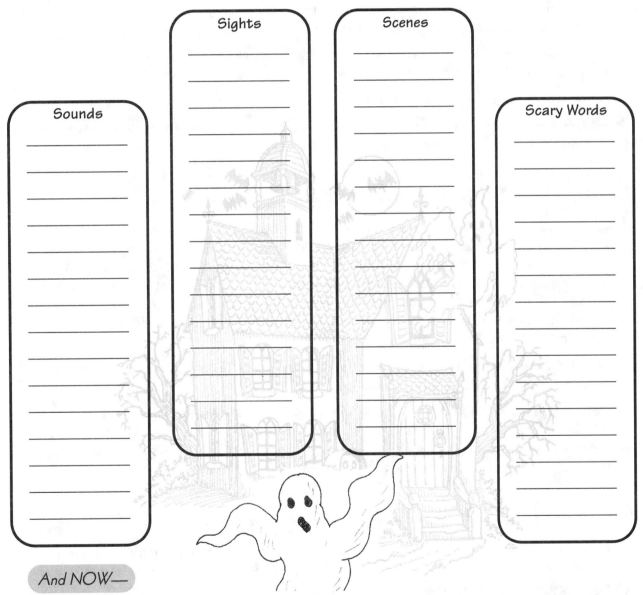

Sights	Scenes

Sounds

Scary Words

And NOW—

Use the details to write a scary story. Imagine telling it at a pajama party, around a campfire, or by candlelight on Halloween night. Work to make your audience shiver!

Did You Hear the One About . . . ?

Students will create original riddles or jokes that have punch lines.

SET THE STAGE

★ Display an assortment of riddle books or joke books students can browse through to stimulate their creativity.

★ Read aloud some riddles or jokes. Before you reveal the endings, give students time to guess the answers or the punch lines.

★ Duplicate and distribute the planner on page 39. Go over the definitions together. Then have students tickle their funnybones by creating original riddles and/or jokes.

★ Allow students to retell riddles or jokes they know, revising them with their own twists.

★ Suggest that students condense the plots of books, films, or TV shows to recast them as riddles or jokes.

GUIDE THE WAY

★ Help students by explaining *puns*, *spoonerisms*, and *Tom Swift-ies*. A *pun* is a riddle or joke based on word play. For example, it would be a pun to call a tiny scratch a *short cut*. (Get it?) A *spoonerism* is the switching of normal sounds in words to form a silly new phrase. For example, did you ever ride a *well-boiled icicle?!* (Get it—a well-oiled bicycle?) A *Tom Swift-y* is an expression (some call it a groaner!) that includes an adverb to characterize how Tom Swift, a fictional character, says something. For example, "I'm so thirsty," said Tom dryly. (Get it?)

★ Tell students that good jokes are short and to the point. If they go on for too long, the audience may fall asleep before the punch line.

> **Delivery!**—*Jokes and riddles are part of oral tradition. That means that they are often told aloud. As you work on your riddles and jokes, read them out loud. Say the words and ideas as if you were a stand-up comic. Are the clues clear? Does the joke have a twist? Does the punch line work?*

FOLLOW IT UP

★ Hold a riddle riot or joke-around—let students take turns sharing their riddles and jokes with small groups or with the class. Pass around a microphone (or something to represent one). Invite guests in for a Funny Friday!

★ Collect students' riddles and jokes in a file box or binder. Present them as warm-ups or to end class meetings. Or use them as offbeat ways to practice punctuation or spelling.

Name: _____

Did You Hear the One About...?

 A *riddle* is a nonsense question that has a clever answer.
A *joke* is a funny story told to make people laugh.
A *punch line* is the last line of a joke or story that makes it funny or surprising.

 Write a riddle you think is clever. Include the answer.

_____

_____

_____

_____

_____

 Write a joke you think is funny. Circle the punch line.

_____

_____

_____

_____

_____

_____

_____

And NOW—

Comedians work hard on their *delivery*—the way they tell riddles or jokes to an audience to get big laughs. Practice delivering the riddle and joke you wrote. Be clever! Be funny! Then try to tickle an audience!

What If . . .?

Students will write responses to hypothetical *what if* situations.

SET THE STAGE

★ Define *suppose* as a verb that means "to imagine, believe, or assume something is true, possible, or might come about." *What if . . . ?* is a simple question to use to get students thinking about suppositions—from realistic possibilities, to outlandish fantasies.

★ Read an excerpt from a story that explores a *what if . . . ?* situation. Consider the genres of adventure, autobiography, fantasy, folklore, or science fiction.

★ Display unusual visual images to spark students' creativity. Look for stimulating examples in magazine ads, in reproductions of fine art, or in whimsical cartoons.

★ Discuss questions like these: *What would the world would be like if something you take for granted suddenly changed dramatically? Can planning ahead fully prepare you for a what if . . . ? situation that comes true?*

★ Duplicate and distribute the *What if . . . ?* planner on page 41.

★ Some students might prefer to write about realistic *what if . . . ?* situations that focus on safety, family issues, human relationships or world or community events.

GUIDE THE WAY

★ Students may be able to develop a *what if . . . ?* situations by imagining that they play the main characters in movies or plays about the events. Challenge them to visualize key scenes, conversations, and examples of how the supposed events would affect them.

★ Help students decide how to begin their stories. Will they provide background about the settings, the characters, and the situations? Will they describe certain moods or tension? Will they jump right into important pieces of action?

> **Anecdote**—*This kind of writing may be called an* anecdote *because it tells a story about an interesting event. You are the main character of this anecdote. Be sure to give all the usual details you'd include in any story. But remember, in an anecdote, you show how you learn a lesson or realize something important.*

FOLLOW IT UP

★ Display completed *What if . . . ?* stories on a bulletin board. You might have students create covers for their pieces that state the *What if . . . ?* supposition to draw readers in.

★ Have students create a series of *What if . . . ?* situations and write each one on a slip of paper. Put them in an envelope. From time to time, select one at random to use for a writing assignment or the basis for an oral presentation.

40

Name: _____

WRITE AWAY!
What If . . .?

🔑 *What if . . . ?* is a question to tempt your cleverness and creativity.
Some *what ifs . . . ?* may come true. Others will never happen.
BUT—*what if* they did*???*

✏️ Pick a *what if . . . ?* situation. Or, think up your own. What if

- ❑ ...a teenager got to be President?
- ❑ ...you awoke, realizing that you'd slept for five years?
- ❑ ...there were no more television?
- ❑ ...a stray dog followed you home from school?
- ❑ ...you were lost in the desert?
- ❑ ...a rock-and-roll band moved in upstairs?
- ❑ ...you found $1,000,000 in your garage?
- ❑ ...food could speak to you?
- ❑ ...your best friend moved away?

_____?

✏️ Think about the *what if . . . ?* happening. Jot down responses to these questions:

⭐ What would change? _____
_____

⭐ How would you feel? _____
_____

⭐ What would you do? _____
_____

⭐ Who would help? _____
_____

And NOW—

Use your responses as you write your *what if . . . ?* story. Be sure to explain the *what if . . . ?*
situation—how it came about, and how it affects you and your world.

Tongue Twisters

Students will create original tongue twisters using alliteration and other sound devices.

> Tom took ten tubas to Tokyo!

SET THE STAGE

★ Define a *tongue twister* as a group of words that is difficult to say quickly or to repeat without error. The best of them make some kind of sense, but should be divinely and devilishly difficult to declaim! Good tongue twisters incorporate clever thinking, reading and writing skills, and a sense of fun.

★ Post a display of assorted tongue twisters students can try to say. Visit a wild and wacky Web site with tons of tricky tongue twisters at:
  http://www.geocities.com/Athens/8136/tonguetwisters.html

★ Explain two techniques students can use to write tongue twisters: *alliteration* and *assonance. Alliteration* is the grouping of words that share the same initial sound, such as, "Tom took ten tubas to Tokyo." *Assonance* is the repetition of the same internal vowel sound, despite different consonants. An example is, "In deep green fields, sweet sheep weep bleakly."

★ Duplicate and distribute the tongue twister planner on page 43.

★ Students may work individually, in pairs, or in small groups to write tongue twisters.

GUIDE THE WAY

★ Encourage students to use a dictionary or thesaurus to expand their options for alliterative and assonant words.

★ Students whose first language is not English can share tongue twisters in their own tongues. Even students who cannot understand the words should be able to appreciate the sounds. You might investigate the "First International Collection of Tongue Twisters" which boasts nearly 1,200 tongue twisters in 58 languages, at:
  http://www.uebersetzung.at/twister/

> **Tangling Terms**—*Is your tongue twister tricky enough? Make it harder by substituting words that tangle tongues, mangle mouths, and trip lips!*

FOLLOW IT UP

★ Challenge students to combine tongue twisters into a tongue-twisting paragraph!

★ Have tongue twister contests in which students attempt to outdo one another at reciting the tongue twisters they have created.

★ Suggest that students illustrate their tongue twisters with sketches, cartoons, or collages.

Name: _____

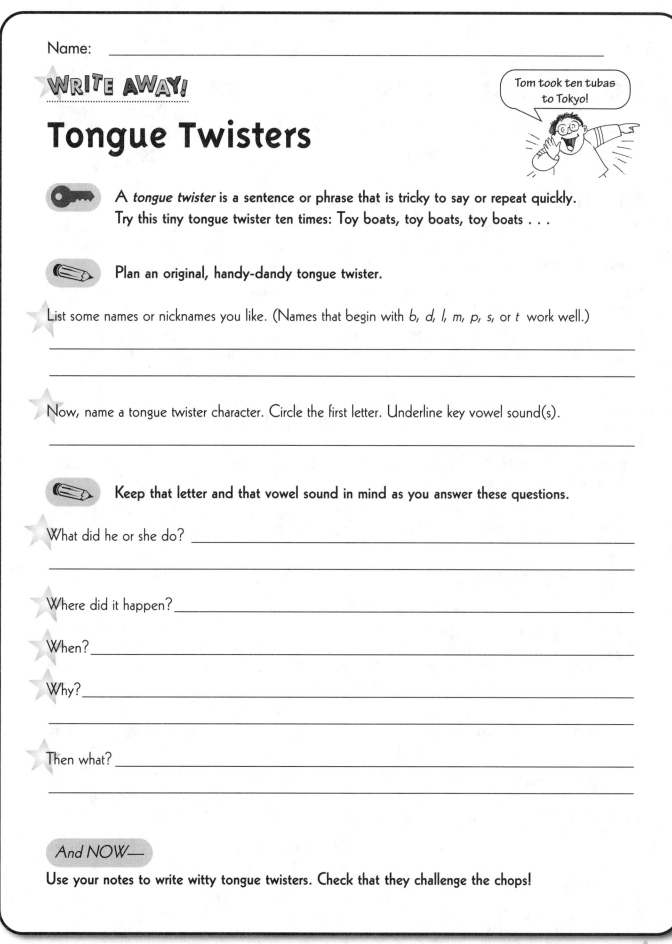

WRITE AWAY!

Tom took ten tubas to Tokyo!

Tongue Twisters

🔑 A *tongue twister* is a sentence or phrase that is tricky to say or repeat quickly. Try this tiny tongue twister ten times: Toy boats, toy boats, toy boats . . .

✏️ Plan an original, handy-dandy tongue twister.

⭐ List some names or nicknames you like. (Names that begin with *b, d, l, m, p, s,* or *t* work well.)

_____

_____

⭐ Now, name a tongue twister character. Circle the first letter. Underline key vowel sound(s).

_____

✏️ Keep that letter and that vowel sound in mind as you answer these questions.

⭐ What did he or she do? _____

_____

⭐ Where did it happen? _____

⭐ When? _____

⭐ Why? _____

_____

⭐ Then what? _____

_____

And NOW—

Use your notes to write witty tongue twisters. Check that they challenge the chops!

Pourquoi Story

Students will write stories that attempt to explain natural phenomena.

SET THE STAGE

★ Explain that *pourquoi* [poor-KWA] is the French word for *why*. Then define a *pourquoi* story as a folkloric tale that tries to explain something in nature, such as why stars twinkle, zebras have stripes, snakes hiss, ice melts, and so on.

★ Read aloud a *pourquoi* tale, for example, one of the Rudyard Kipling *Just So Stories* or *Why Mosquitoes Buzz in People's Ears: A West African Tale* by Verna Aardema.

★ Discuss questions like these: *Why would people make up stories to explain natural events? Who might be an audience for a* pourquoi *story? Which do you prefer—the scientific truth or a creative explanation of a natural wonder?*

★ Display pictures of unusual animals, plants, and geological features, as well as images of people of all ages, expressions, and cultures, to spark ideas for *pourquoi* stories.

★ Duplicate and distribute the *pourquoi* planner on page 45. You may want students to begin their first drafts on that page, or save it for a final draft. Students may use their own beginnings, if they wish.

★ You might have groups collaborate on *pourquoi* stories, or assign a particular phenomenon to a group of students so they can compare and contrast their stories.

GUIDE THE WAY

★ Like any story, a *pourquoi* story needs a plot. A writer should first set the scene—time, place, characters, and a basic conflict. Then he or she needs rising action to develop interest or suspense. Next, a writer builds toward the climax, or high point, where the problem is solved. Finally, she or he brings the story to a conclusion that explains the phenomenon and answers any lingering questions.

★ Before students can write *pourquoi* stories, they'll need time to figure out the narrative elements of plot, characters, and setting. Suggest that they muse about their ideas on their own, talk with a partner, or freewrite.

> *Lively Dialogue—In some* pourquoi *stories, creatures or objects that cannot speak in real life may talk! If you use dialogue in your* pourquoi *story, be sure to identify who is speaking. Start a new paragraph each time the speaker changes. Put quotation marks around the exact words spoken.*

FOLLOW IT UP

★ Some students might want to act out *pourquoi* stories, or tell them with puppets.

★ Invite musical learners to create song lyrics that support their tales.

Name: _____

Pourquoi Story

🔑 A *pourquoi* story is a tale that explains something in nature.
Pourquoi stories can be serious or funny. They can seem sensible or fantastic.
Most of all, they are entertaining. Some of them teach a lesson.

✏️ Pick something in nature to explain. Think of a title like one of these:

How the _____ Got Its _____

Why the _____ Has _____

How _____ Came To Be _____

✏️ Start your *pourquoi* story here. Use extra paper if you need to.

Long, long ago, before there were _____

or _____

_____

_____

_____

_____

_____

_____

_____

_____

And that's why, from then on, _____

_____

_____ !

And NOW—

Illustrate your *pourquoi* story. Share it with younger children.

My Sci-Fi

Students will create original science fiction stories.

SET THE STAGE

★ Define *science fiction* (or *sci fi*) as stories about life in the future or in distant worlds. Science fiction blends known scientific fact with visionary ideas about how things might be someday. It may include amazing technology that we only dream about today.

★ Read excerpts from classic science fiction, such as *A Wrinkle in Time* by Madeleine L'Engle, *Dolphin Island* by Arthur C. Clarke, *Farmer in the Sky* by Robert A. Heinlein, or "All Summer in a Day" by Ray Bradbury. Or talk about famous science fiction films or TV shows students may have seen, such as *Star Wars* or *Third Rock From the Sun*.

★ Display pictures of technological advances that are part of our every day life today such as computers, airplanes, underwater cameras, freeze-dried foods, and mobile phones. To emphasize the nature of science fiction, tell students that a generation or two back, such ideas would have been laughed at as absolutely ridiculous!

★ Discuss questions like these: *What appeals to you about science fiction? Did you ever want to travel to outer space or into the future? What do you imagine doing or finding there? Do you think that people in the future will be different than they are today?*

★ Duplicate and distribute the plot diagram on page 47. Help students understand that the plot diagram is a tool that can help them plan what will happen in their stories.

★ Another way to plan plot is to jot down ideas, events, or situations on index cards. Students can then put the cards into a sensible order and use the sequence to construct their stories.

GUIDE THE WAY

★ Explain that some science fiction tries to warn us of future problems such as dangerous pollution or extinction of animal species. You might guide students to consider taking such a stand, if they wish.

> **Data!**—*Science fiction needs some science words such as* gravity, data, *or* force field. *Look through science books for ideas you can use to jazz up your story and appeal to futuristic readers. You may not be able to travel to outer space yourself, but there's no limit on where your imagination can go!*

FOLLOW IT UP

★ Have students read science fiction books and write readers' responses to them.

★ Have students reframe their science fiction stories as radio plays.

Name: _____

WRITE AWAY!
My Sci-Fi

🔑 *Science fiction (or sci-fi)* is imaginary stories about the future or life on distant planets.

✏️ Use this page to plan a sci-fi story. Follow the arrows to plan a thrilling plot.

RISING ACTION & CONFLICT

_____
_____
_____
_____
_____
_____
_____
_____
_____

CLIMAX

_____
_____
_____
_____
_____
_____
_____
_____

SET THE SCENE

_____
_____
_____
_____
_____
_____

FALLING ACTION

_____
_____
_____
_____

START

WRAP-UP

_____
_____
_____
_____

And NOW—

Use your ideas to write a science fiction story.

Dastardly Deeds

Students will write original mystery stories.

SET THE STAGE

★ Define a *mystery* as a story that contains a puzzle to be solved. *Dastardly* means "sneaky, cowardly, or evil."

★ Describe some hallmarks of classic mysteries, such as *clues* (hints), *suspects* (people who might be guilty), *red herrings* (misleading/distracting clues), and *detectives* (those who try to crack the case).

★ Help students understand these elements by identifying them in well-known mysteries or "whodunnits." Read excerpts from one of the *Encyclopedia Brown* mysteries by Donald J. Sobol, or another age-appropriate mystery story. Pause as you read to encourage response.

★ Discuss questions like these: *What makes a mystery puzzling? What do you like best about reading or solving mysteries? What sorts of characters do you usually find in mysteries? Why do you think authors drop clues or hints in a mystery?*

★ Duplicate and distribute the Whodunnit? planner on page 49. Tell students that they can use it to plan a mystery story by focusing on three key elements that can establish a villain's guilt: *motive* (Why?), *means* (How?), and *opportunity* (When?).

★ Present some titles, or title templates, to stimulate students' creativity. Rely on tried-and-true forms, such as "The Case of the [Laughing Musician]," "C is for [Clue]," "What Became of [the Necklace]?" or "The Mystery of the [Strange Dog]."

GUIDE THE WAY

★ Suggest that students talk with each other to construct mysteries, one of the hardest genres they may try. Allow them ample time to plan, think, and work out kinks.

★ Help students plan their mysteries. They must decide on the dastardly deeds (and the motive and means), the victims, the suspects, and some clues to drop along the way. And, of course, they must figure out how the crimes are eventually solved, and by whom.

> ***Prepositional Phrases***—*Details of setting are important in a mystery. You'll want to use lots of details to help readers answer questions like* Where? When? *and* In what way? *Use prepositional phrases, such as* on the window ledge, between the walls, inside the safe, past midnight, *or* outside the dungeon.

FOLLOW IT UP

★ Have students share their mysteries by reading them aloud, or by tape-recording them for classmates to enjoy. Suggest that authors stop before revealing the solutions to see if the audience can unravel the mysteries.

Name: _____

Dastardly Deeds

🔑 A *mystery* is a story that offers a puzzle to solve. A mystery needs a problem, a hunt, and a solution—plus clever clues and shady characters.

✏️ Use this planner to develop an idea for a mystery story.

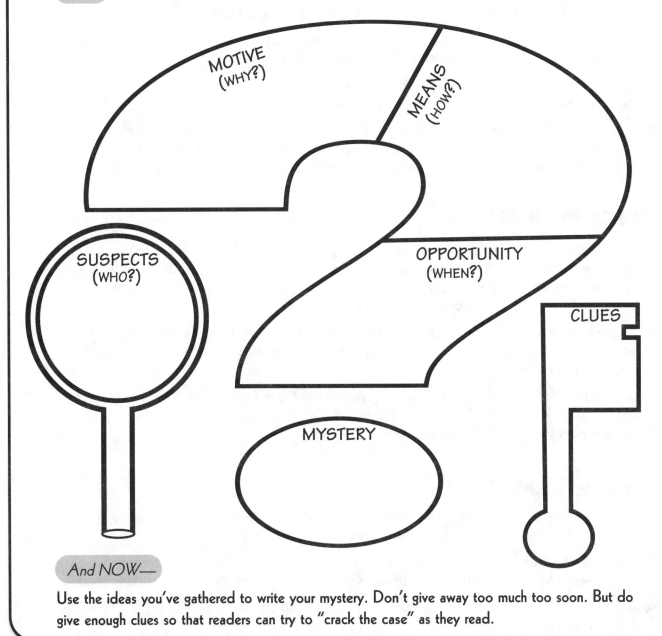

MOTIVE
(WHY?)

MEANS
(HOW?)

SUSPECTS
(WHO?)

OPPORTUNITY
(WHEN?)

CLUES

MYSTERY

And NOW—

Use the ideas you've gathered to write your mystery. Don't give away too much too soon. But do give enough clues so that readers can try to "crack the case" as they read.

Comic Strip

Students will develop brief comic strips that includes their own drawings and dialogue.

Snowman Sam

I could really cool off with a nice cold glass of lemonade!

SET THE STAGE

★ Display examples of popular comic strips from local newspapers. Be sure to select examples that have more than one frame.

★ Discuss questions like these: *What makes comic strips appealing? Which comic strips do you enjoy? What do you like best about your favorite ones? Which is more important to you—the art or the words? Do you prefer human characters or non-human ones?*

★ Duplicate and distribute the comic strip information and organizer on page 51. Tell students that they will use this to develop, draw, and write dialogue for comic strips.

★ As a variation, provide actual comic strips with the words deleted. Invite students to make up new words to fit the existing drawings.

★ As another alternative, suggest that students create "gag panels"—single-frame funnies, such as "Dennis the Menace" or "Ziggy." They might attach brief character sketches to give background on the characters in the gag panels.

GUIDE THE WAY

★ Point out that students need not possess great art skill to draw comic strips. Encourage them to draw the simple characters and background details they need, but remind them that a comic strip tells a story. So, like any story, they need to provide a setting, characters, and a brief problem or plot.

★ Suggest that students visualize short episodes or anecdotes that they can turn into comic strips. Emphasize that there's no room for lots of details; students should be concise and clear.

> **Casual Talk**—*In a comic strip, it's okay to use informal language or slang. Make characters speak as real people might. You can use words like* hooray! *or* hmmm, *or sound effects words such as* Splat! Gasp! Yikes! *or* Pow!

FOLLOW IT UP

★ Post students' comic strips on a bulletin board, or scan them into your classroom computer so they can be posted on the Internet.

★ Make a collection of favorite comic strips. Invite students to write fan letters or responses to cartoonists they like, in care of the newspapers that publish their works.

★ Extend by having students create political or editorial cartoons that give their opinions on current issues.

Name: _____

WRITE AWAY!
Comic Strip

 You know what comic strips are. Do you know these words about them?

Frames: The boxes in a comic strip; also called *panels.*

Talk bubble: Cloudlike shape that holds the words a character says.
Talk bubbles have pointers that aim toward the character that says them.

Thought bubble: Like a talk bubble, but the pointer—a row of dots—means that the words are thoughts, not speech.

Use the frames below to plan a comic strip. If you need more frames, get another copy of this page or draw your own frames on larger paper.

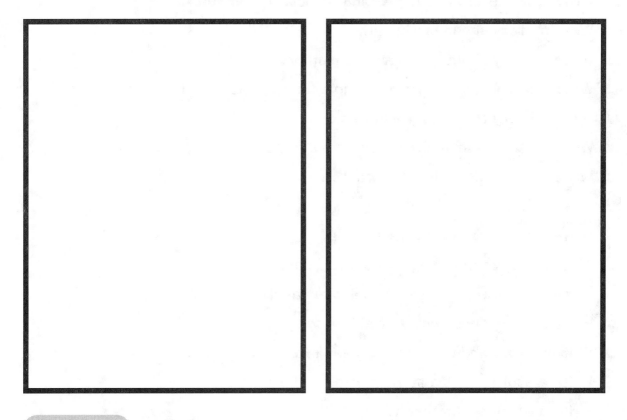

And NOW—

Do a final draft of your comic strip. Be sure the words sound like ones the characters would actually say or think. You can include sound effects words, background details, and an introduction panel, if you like.

More Ideas for Narrative Writing

❑ Write a story about a clown.

❑ Write a true story about something you did that made you proud.

❑ Write a true story about looking after a younger child.

❑ Write a true story about somebody in your family.

❑ Write a true story about an emergency.

❑ Write a true story about something that made you laugh a lot.

❑ Write a true story about a good plan that went wrong.

❑ Write a true story about being sick.

❑ Write a true story about meeting somebody famous.

❑ Write a story about moving away.

❑ Write a story about your earliest memory.

❑ Write a story about learning to do something for the first time.

❑ Write a story that has a surprise ending.

❑ Write a story that has an alien as a character.

❑ Write a story with animal characters.

❑ Write a sad story.

❑ Write a story about making friends.

❑ Write a story that takes place on a boat.

❑ Write a story that takes place in the past.

❑ Write a story about being afraid of something.

❑ Write a story about winning a great prize.

❑ Write a story about a terrible meal.

❑ Write a story about time travel.

❑ Write a story about a cave.

❑ Write and draw a multipanel comic strip about a hero.

The Big Book of Ready-to-Go Writing Lessons • Scholastic Professional Books

Write to Inform

The goal of **expository** writing is to give information. Expository writing may convey ideas, provide step-by-step directions, or explain how to complete a task. Expository writing must present facts and details in an orderly way; it should be extremely clear and informative.

Techniques of expository writing include the use of transition words such as *first*, *then*, or *finally*, and graphic organizers such as tables, charts, graphs, or diagrams. Expository writing needs well-structured paragraphs with topic sentences supported by details; it should be geared to meet the needs of a specific audience.

Evaluation Tips

There are many ways to evaluate students' expository writing. Here are some broad points to consider as you judge some or all of the writing activities in this section of the book:

Does the expository piece have—

- ❏ A stated purpose or clear focus?
- ❏ A sensible plan of organization?
- ❏ A beginning, middle, and end?
- ❏ Paragraphs with main ideas and supporting details?
- ❏ Effective transitions?
- ❏ Thorough explanations?
- ❏ Precise language?
- ❏ Accurate definitions?

- ❏ Is the piece complete?
- ❏ Does it allow readers to get information clearly?
- ❏ Does it show planning and follow-through?
- ❏ Is the word choice thoughtful, precise, and informative?
- ❏ How are the mechanics (grammar, usage, spelling, punctuation)?

But Why?

Students will write clear, simple definitions or explanations aimed at younger children.

Why the Earth Needs the Sun and the Moon

SET THE STAGE

★ Display pictures of foods, tools, animals, people at work, and so on, that might make young children ask questions. Examples include an artichoke, a telescope, a kangaroo, a crescent moon, a flock of birds flying in a V formation, a submarine, and so on.

★ Read aloud some definitions from a dictionary for young children. Or read an entry from a children's encyclopedia. Talk about the importance of using clear language, short sentences, and examples to help young children grasp new ideas.

★ Discuss questions like these: *Can you remember questions you asked when you were little? Who explained things to you? Who is the best person who explains things you don't know? What is it about the way that person explains things that is so effective?*

★ Duplicate and distribute the organizer on page 55. Students can use it to compose their definitions or explanations.

★ Ask kindergarten or first-grade teachers to list some questions young children have asked them, or some ideas they know their students want to know more about. Present the list to students to stimulate their prewriting ideas.

GUIDE THE WAY

★ Suggest that students put themselves in the place of a younger child, and aim their definitions or explanations accordingly. For instance, to tell what a rainbow is, they might realize that they should review color names or use simpler words like *curve* instead of *arc*.

★ Point out that a good way to define or explain something is to include an example that supports the main idea. For instance, to explain what a mammal is, a writer might say that mammals have hair or fur, like people, dogs, tigers, and squirrels do.

> ***Editorial Choice***—*To present information to young children, you don't have to include every last detail. It's more important that what you do say is clear and in order. Have you used simple sentences? Have you used words that young children will know? Have you broken big ideas into smaller ones? Are the details clear and in order?*

FOLLOW IT UP

★ Have students share their work with younger children in your school.

★ Suggest that your students use this retelling or simplifying approach to help them learn new terms in content areas, such as science, social studies, or health.

Name: _____

 WRITE AWAY!
But Why?

Why the Earth Needs the Sun and the Moon

 A *definition* tells the meaning of a word or phrase.
An *explanation* tells who or why something is, or how it works.
Definitions and explanations can be complicated, but they don't have to be.

 Pick an idea below to define or explain. Or think up your own.

Why do some people wear glasses?   Where does the sun go at night?
What does a plumber do?   Why don't seals get cold?
How does water turn into ice?   What is a rainbow?
When do fish sleep?   Why do people yawn?
What do your lungs do?   Who names streets and roads?

 Define or explain the idea. Keep it simple. Keep it clear.

_____

_____

_____

_____

_____

_____

_____

And NOW—

What kind of picture, illustration, or model would help a young child better understand the idea you're explaining or defining? Add it to your written work. Now share your work with a young child. Notice the child's response. How could you rework your definition or explanation to make it better?

How-To Instructions

Students will write clear sets of instructions.

SET THE STAGE

★ Discuss real-life situations in which people follow written directions. Examples might include cooking from a recipe, filling out an official form, applying for a job, using a travel guide, reading a train schedule, or learning the rules of a board game.

★ Display some how-to instructions that come with toys, furniture, models, or other items that need assembly. Which ones are clear? Which are confusing?

★ Review the idea of *sequence*, or the order of things.

★ Talk about ideas like these: *What features make directions easy to follow? What kinds of visual cues help organize a written set of instructions? How do the cues help? What strategies can you use to check that you have presented instructions in the best possible order?*

★ Brainstorm the key elements of some how-to tasks, such as how to feed a dog, build a snow fort, program a VCR, change batteries in a toy, eat corn on the cob, use an egg beater, make a braid, look up a word in the dictionary, wash out paint brushes, and so on.

★ Duplicate and distribute the step-by-step organizer on page 57. Students can use this form to get started and/or to present final drafts of their how-to instructions.

★ You may want to focus the task by guiding students into broad how-to categories, such as how to play a game, fix a food, build a model, or research something.

GUIDE THE WAY

★ Review words and phrases that indicate sequence and help writers provide clear, step-by-step instructions. Examples include *first, next, then, now, finally, begin by, move on to, after that,* or *conclude by.*

★ Indicate useful visual cues that separate steps into easy-to-read "chunks." These include numbers, letters, bullets, check marks, or other icons at the start of each new step. Show examples of these cues from written sources (including this book!).

> ***That's an Order!***—*It's great to use words that suggest order, but be sure that the order you use makes sense. Read over your instructions to check order words. If you rearrange steps, you may need to rearrange order words, too.*

FOLLOW IT UP

★ Have students exchange how-to instructions and try to follow them.

★ Challenge students to rewrite existing how-to instructions to make them better.

★ Create humorous how-to instructions such as "How to Get Your Cat to Eat Your Broccoli," or "How to Get Your Kid Brother to Do Your Chores."

Name: _____

WRITE AWAY!
How-To Instructions

🔑 *Instructions* are rules, orders, or directions to follow.
A set of instructions tells everything you need to make or do something.
The steps are in order, from beginning to end.

✏️ Use this step-by-step organizer to create a set of instructions.

⭐ HOW TO _____

- _____

_____

- _____

_____

- _____

_____

- _____

_____

- _____

_____

And NOW—

Check your instructions. Are they given in order? Did you include everything that is important?
Would it help to add order words? Visual cues? Diagrams or sketches? Can you follow your own
instructions? Try it to be sure! Revise as needed.

Funny Foods

Students will create mock recipes with silly ingredients, and give cooking instructions.

SET THE STAGE

★ Display cookbooks with easy-to-follow recipes for students to browse through.

★ Read these two lines from Shakespeare's *Macbeth*, about some items three witches put into a cauldron to make a potion: "Eye of newt and toe of frog/Wool of bat and tongue of dog . . . " Or read any version of the famous folktale *Stone Soup*.

★ Discuss questions like these: *What information do all recipes include? In what ways is the information usually given? Have you ever tried to follow a recipe? What happened?*

★ Duplicate and distribute the recipe planner on page 59. Tell students to use it to create a silly dish with wild ingredients. They record the information as if it were a real recipe.

★ Students might need prompts to get their creative juices flowing. Suggest that they start with standard fare, but add crazy twists. What about Artist's Stew, Toothpaste Cake, Mud & Mushroom Casserole, Plumber's Pizza, Pebble Pie, or Spooky Salad?

GUIDE THE WAY

★ Encourage creativity with a dash of silliness. Allow students to use outlandish ingredients, stomach-churning combinations, and ridiculous cooking techniques!

★ Despite the inherent humor, this writing task requires students to think. They must consider how to order the steps, how to present ingredients (with measurements!), and how many the revolting recipe may serve! Also, recipes for younger cooks often include a list of utensils (mixing bowls, measuring spoons, egg beater, and so on) to help novice cooks gather what they need *before* they get elbow-deep in goo!

> **Smart Set-Up**—*It makes sense to list ingredients in the order you expect cooks to use them. Revise and edit your recipe so that the ingredients list and the cooking steps make sense together.*

FOLLOW IT UP

★ Have students collect the recipes into a kooky cookbook.

★ Encourage students to use some of the recipes to role-play a mock cooking show. Classmates can write reviews of the performances! [But no food fights!]

★ Extend by challenging students to write out recipes for real, simple yet edible dishes.

Name: _____

Funny Foods

 A *recipe* is a set of instructions for preparing and cooking food. Here's your chance to invent a wacky recipe for creative (and zany!) cooks!

Think about a dizzy dish to make. List its ingredients (with amounts!). Tell what utensils to gather. Then give step-by-steps instructions for how to prepare the dish.

Recipe Name: _____

Ingredients list:

_____

_____

_____   Utensils:
                                          ....
_____

_____

Steps:

_____

_____

_____

_____

_____

_____

_____

_____

_____

_____

And NOW—

Write a paragraph that introduces the dish and suggests other foods that might go well with it.

Closer Look Log

Students will focus on a specific environment for 5 minutes.

SET THE STAGE

★ Define the word *observation* as the careful watching of something. Most observers use their eyes first, but they can also use their other senses—touch, hearing, taste, and smell—when appropriate.

★ Brainstorm to list things students might closely observe for 5 minutes. Guide them to think of in-class, at-home, and outside options. For example, they could spend 5 minutes observing sparrows at a bird bath, or traffic to and from an anthill or nest. They might observe a spider at its web, a caterpillar on a leaf, the class hamster in its cage, and so on. Emphasize that each observer will stay put and focus on a small, fixed area. Remind students to be careful when touching, smelling, or tasting. They may use their sight to infer how these senses might be affected.

★ Discuss questions like these: *How can you be a good observer? What kinds of things would you write down? How can drawing help? What if you don't notice much of anything at first?*

★ Duplicate and distribute the Closer Look Log on page 61.

★ Students might also use a sensory details chart (see p. 25). You might have pairs or trios observe the same spot so they can pool their notes later.

★ As an alternative, have students make a simple four-sided frame out of paper strips. They can place their frames on the ground and observe what is within the frames, as well as what comes and goes through the space.

GUIDE THE WAY

★ Set ground rules for ways to observe nature without disturbing it. Focus on keeping silent, staying still, and not upsetting a natural habitat.

★ Encourage students to jot notes, not necessarily full sentences. Sketches can help, too.

> **Come to Order**—*You'll probably record what you observe in time order. But when you write your paragraph, you might prefer to present details in order of importance. It's your choice. Use the plan of order that you think readers will find more interesting.*

FOLLOW IT UP

★ Have students share their pieces orally or bind them into a group observation log.

★ Invite students to write creative pieces about what they *might observe* if they were to do the same activity in the same spot at night or in a different season.

Name: _____

★ WRITE AWAY!
Closer Look Log

🔑 A *log* is a place to write down whatever
you observe. This includes what you see, hear,
feel, smell, and taste (*only if* it's safe to feel, smell, and taste).

✏️ Pick a small spot to observe for 5 minutes.
Look quite closely, and stay alert!
More goes on than you may notice at first!

_____
_____
_____
_____
_____
_____

Observation Spot: _____

_____

_____

Sketch here:

Time: _____

And NOW—

Use the details you gathered to write a paragraph. Give information about what you observed
during the 5 minutes. Include the big stuff and the little stuff.

Sky Writing

Students will present information in brief, concise form.

SET THE STAGE

★ Explain to students that *skywriting* is the process of spelling words with smoke, one letter at a time, in the sky. Skywriting presents information to people on the ground. Skywriting is done by pilots who use special planes, equipment, and techniques to make the huge letters readable and clear. Some skywriting is done by a single plane; other skywriting is done by a team of pilots.

★ Remind students of (or show a video clip of) the scene from *The Wizard of Oz*, in which the Wicked Witch of the West sky-writes, "Surrender, Dorothy!"

★ Discuss questions like these: *Have you ever seen skywriting? What kind of information is given this way? What messages might someone want to skywrite? Why should sky-written messages be short? What happens to the messages after a few moments?*

★ Duplicate and distribute the cloud organizer on page 63.

★ As an alternative, students might create messages that small, low-flying planes can drag behind them, or create informational bumper stickers.

GUIDE THE WAY

★ Help students think of important pieces of information that would be exciting enough to warrant skywritten messages. Since skywriting is expensive, tricky to do, and depends on clear weather, it isn't done very often. But the sky's the limit here!

★ Spelling counts! Help students proofread their messages so that each word is spelled correctly and any necessary punctuation is included.

> **Every Word Counts!**—*A skywriting message must be short. Take the time to pick the best words you can think of to say exactly what you want to say. Is your message clear? Will people know what you mean? Did you spell all the words right?*

FOLLOW IT UP

★ Have students create their own skywritten messages using a series of thumbprints. They may dip their thumbs in tempera paint, chalkdust, or press their thumbs onto stamp pads. Students can imagine each thumbprint as a blast of smoke from the plane as it creates the individual letters of the message.

★ Visit the Web site at **http://www.skytypers.com/skywriting.html**.

★ For a social studies connection, help students learn how smoke was used to send signals and messages long before there were telephones and radios.

WRITE AWAY!
Sky Writing

Happy 4th!

🔑 Skywriting is just what it sounds like—writing in the sky!
Think of a message you might like to skywrite. Keep it short!

✏️ Write your message here. Spelling counts!

And NOW—

Write a letter to a skywriting pilot. Tell what message you'd like to see in the air. Tell what it's for, who you hope will see it, and why it's important. Include other details such as what colors to use, when to skywrite, and anything else you'd want the pilot to know.

Solve a Problem

Students will present problems and develop reasonable solutions.

SET THE STAGE

★ Define a problem as a difficult situation that must be figured out or overcome. Point out that one reason to give information is to explain the problem, provide details about it, and offer a solution. Such writing requires facts and/or examples.

★ Read an excerpt from a story in which a character faces a problem. Have students identify the problem and propose possible solutions to it.

★ Discuss questions like these: *What factors make a problem hard to describe? Hard to solve? Have you ever faced a problem that you had to solve on your own? How can you judge whether a solution might work before you actually try it?*

★ Duplicate and distribute the problem planner on page 65.

★ Some students might focus on problems that involve themselves, another individual, the class, the school, or the community. Others may consider problems that affect the nation or world. Encourage students to pick problems that concern them.

GUIDE THE WAY

★ Explain that everyone faces problems, large and small. Brainstorm to list realistic ones to explore. Examples might include how to keep a promise; how to complete a hard task; how to get along with a grumpy neighbor; how to memorize something; how to break a bad habit; or how to cheer up someone.

★ Tell students that writing about problems is like any kind of writing: you don't always get it right on the first try! Guide students to be flexible. If solutions don't seem to work, urge them to think of other possibilities. If *that* doesn't work, they might narrow the problems or the focus of their solutions.

> **Stick With It!**—*Solving problems isn't easy. Solving one problem might create a new one. But don't give up! Role-play your plan with a partner or in your mind. Think of what might work, even if it won't bring a perfect solution. Or try a new approach.*

FOLLOW IT UP

★ Send noteworthy problem-and-solution essays to the editor of the local paper, to the appropriate government representative or agency, or to a publication that prints works by young writers. Or post them on the Internet to encourage give-and-take responses.

★ Invite students to evaluate one another's solutions. Based on the feedback, ask students: *If you had it to do over, would you propose the same solution? Explain.*

Name: _____

WRITE AWAY!
Solve a Problem

🔑   You can solve many problems with a good plan.

✏️   Pick a problem you'd like to solve. _____

_____

Use this problem planner to help you figure out a solution.

⭐ What's wrong? What should change? _____

_____

_____

⭐ What should be done now? _____

_____

⭐ What can be done over time? _____

_____

⭐ How can you get others to join in? _____

_____

⭐ What good things might come of your plan? _____

_____

_____

⭐ What might go wrong? _____

_____

_____

And NOW—

Write an essay that describes your problem. Explain your ideas for a solution. Tell what you hope
will happen. Be sure to include warnings about what might go wrong.

Science Q & A

Students will select science questions, and provide answers.

⭐ SET THE STAGE

★ Tell students that *Q & A* means questions and answers. It refers to a style of presenting information.

★ Display books on an array of science topics of interest to students, such as ocean life, weather, volcanoes, astronomy, magnets, computers, aviation, electricity, and so on.

★ Invite students to jot on index cards or sticky notes science questions they've wondered about, such as: *How do radios work? Why don't whales drown? Why did dinosaurs become extinct? What makes stars twinkle? How do batteries make power? What causes a sneeze? Why do some people have allergies? Who first invented eye glasses?*

★ Collect students' science questions, and then distribute them at random, or allow students to choose a question of interest to them. This question will form the basis of a science Q & A report.

★ Duplicate and distribute the gathering grid on page 67, which students can use to help arrange the information they need to answer the question.

★ Pairs or groups of students might brainstorm together to generate broad topics from which they can formulate specific questions.

⭐ GUIDE THE WAY

★ Talk about the kinds of resources students can use to help them answer their questions, such as books, encyclopedias, Internet sites, magazine articles, or first-hand interviews.

★ Help students plan how best to present their information, once they have collected it. They might prepare written reports with illustrations or graphs. They might use question-and-answer formats; they might plan talks enhanced by pertinent visual aids.

Connections—*Don't just give facts in a list. Link information in a sensible way. Make details flow so that the report is interesting, clear, and to the point. Think about using a cool quotation or a chart, or ending with a question that will make readers want more!*

⭐ FOLLOW IT UP

★ Have students share their Q & A papers orally, post them on the Internet, or display them on a science Q & A bulletin board.

★ Work with the science teacher to plan a unit that addresses some of the issues that generated the most interest among students. Plan ways to link research and writing with listening, speaking, learning, and evaluating.

Name: _____

WRITE AWAY!
Science Q & A

🔑 Q & A means Questions and Answers. A good way to learn about a science topic is to ask questions—and then find answers to them.

✏️ Use the table below to plan a Q & A report. Fill in facts you need—and where you got them.

QUESTION: _____

	Facts/Details	Key Terms	Resources
What?			
Where?			
Why?			
How?			
Who?			
Visuals:			

⭐ Related Questions:

_____ ?

_____ ?

_____ ?

And NOW—

Use the facts you gathered to write a science Q & A report. Begin by asking the question(s) that got you started. Then answer it with as many details as you need. Make the report clear, helpful, and full of information.

Extra! Extra!

Students will write news articles to provide information.

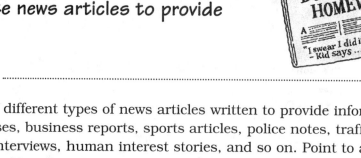

★ Display examples of different types of news articles written to provide information, such as press releases, business reports, sports articles, police notes, traffic advisories, weather forecasts, interviews, human interest stories, and so on. Point to an article and show examples of *headline, lead and body.*

★ Discuss questions like these: *What makes a news article different from other kinds of writing? How can you tell the difference between current news and old news? What kinds of newspaper articles do you like to read? Which ones do you avoid, and why? What do you find in the lead of a newspaper article? What belongs in the body of the article?*

★ Duplicate and distribute the reporter's log on page 69.

★ Some students might create press releases for upcoming events. Others may wish to write human interest stories that would appeal to kids their age.

GUIDE THE WAY ★

★ Go over the purpose of the *lead*, the *body*, and the *wrap-up* of a news article. You might compare these parts to the *introduction, body,* and *conclusion* of a regular essay.

★ Help students understand the value of answering the Five W's in the lead of the news article: *Who? What? Where? When? Why?* (or *How?*). A good article will provide this information in just a few sentences. As the article continues, a reporter can add important information to expand on the Five W's.

★ Remind students that a news article should emphasize facts, not opinions.

★ To gather their information, students can conduct interviews, observe events, or rely on second-hand reports from reliable sources.

> **Headline**—*A headline is like a catchy title for a news article. Reporters usually write the headline last, but it appears first. A headline doesn't have to be a full sentence, but it usually has a subject and verb. It grabs readers by being clever or dramatic. It can grab them by including famous names or well-known places. It can ask a question.*

FOLLOW IT UP

★ Have students work together to produce a class newspaper that has a variety of articles including editorials, advice columns, news stories, human interest features, and so on.

★ Have students role-play the jobs of reporters to gather news about upcoming school or community events. Guide them to write articles for an audience of kids their age.

WRITE AWAY!
Extra! Extra!

 A news story tells of a recent event that is interesting, important, or unusual.

Use this reporter's log to plan a news story. Put the main facts in the *lead*. Next, give key details. Then, add other details that may be helpful. Last, add information that would be good to include *if* there's enough space.

Lead: _____

_____

_____

Key Details: _____

_____

_____

_____

Helpful to Know: _____

_____

_____

_____

If There's Room: _____

_____

_____

_____

And NOW—

Write your news story. Supply all main facts and details in order of importance. Finally, write a headline for your story. Make it catchy, but don't give away too much!

Rules of the Game

Students will provide information in the form of sets of rules for playing games.

⭐ SET THE STAGE

★ Talk about the different ways people learn how to play new games.

★ Display sets of rules for playing games. Invite students to compare and contrast the written rules to find examples of what is effective and what is confusing.

★ Discuss questions like these: *Have you ever tried to learn to play a game by reading the rules yourself? What is hard about reading rules? What makes a set of rules clear? What is confusing? Is it better to have more rules or fewer rules? Should you explain what to do in every possible situation?*

★ Duplicate and distribute the rules planner on page 71.

★ It may work best for students to write sets of rules for games they know well. You might have them play the games once or twice with notebooks at hand in which they write down key details for the sets of rules.

⭐ GUIDE THE WAY

★ One way students can begin is by listing rules, without regard to order. When they think they have all the rules, they can revise or rework their lists to achieve a complete and proper order.

★ Emphasize the importance of presenting the ordered rules in an easy-to-follow format. You might suggest that students number the rules or use graphic icons to make the list visually appealing.

★ Suggest the use of sequence words and phrases, such as *first, then, next,* and *finally*.

> **Test It!**—*Ask a classmate to read the rules you write. Are they clear? Are they in order? If the reader is confused, maybe you need to explain something better. If the reader has to ask questions, maybe you left out something.*

⭐ FOLLOW IT UP

★ Hold a games session in which students bring in games that they know, along with the rules they have written. Divide the class into groups that can learn to play the games.

★ Extend by having students create or invent new games and write the sets of rules.

Name: _____

★ WRITE AWAY!
Rules of the Game

🔑 In a game, *rules* are the directions for how to play. Good rules are clear and in order.

✏️ Use this planner for a set of rules to a game you like to play. You may have more, or fewer, numbered steps.

★ Name of the Game: _____

★ Object of the Game: _____

★ Number of Players: _____

★ Equipment/Pieces: _____
_____

★ To Play:

1. _____
_____

2. _____
_____

3. _____
_____

4. _____
_____

★ The game ends when _____
_____

And NOW—

Revise and edit the rules. Use extra paper, if you need it. Be sure you've included everything. Are the rules clear? Are they complete and in order? Let the games begin!

We'll Call You

Students will convey information in the form of rejection letters.

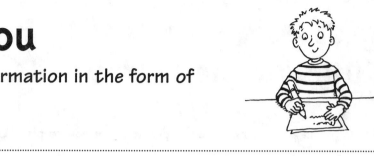

SET THE STAGE

★ Tell students that a *rejection* is a formal way to say no. Talk about situations in which someone might get a rejection letter. Examples include students' rejections from schools they hope to attend; actors' rejections for parts in a play; writers' rejections from magazines that do not wish to publish their stories; or job applicants' rejections for desired positions.

★ Explain that while rejection is always disappointing, a rejection letter can be written in a positive way and can offer encouragement. It can highlight good points and mention areas of weakness that the person can work to improve in the future.

★ Discuss questions like these: *Have you ever had to give someone disappointing news? What would you want someone to tell you if they were writing you a rejection letter? How can you express disappointing news without making the person feel bad?*

★ Duplicate and distribute the letter shell on page 73. Help students think of situations where they might have to write rejection letters. For instance, they could imagine interviewing people for jobs (dog-walker, house painter, piano teacher, and so on.), think about the skills they would look for and what would lead them to reject applicants.

★ Students might role-play job interviews, auditions, or other kinds of competitive situations. They can have a "post-mortem" in which they discuss why someone was rejected for a job, for an art show, for a place on the gymnastics team, and so on. Students can then use the points made in the talk to guide them as they compose their letters.

GUIDE THE WAY

★ Help students plan rejection letters with clear beginnings, middles, and ends. The beginning should break the news directly. The middle might include an honest evaluation of the person's merit, describe the competition, or both. The end might give tips for future success, encouragement and offer thanks for effort or interest.

★ Review the typical parts of any business letter: the heading, inside address, greeting, body, closing, and signature.

> **Tone**—*According to an old saying, "It's not what you say, it's how you say it." This is very true in a rejection letter. Keep the letter natural, but a bit formal. Express the disappointing news gently. Be tactful, be honest. Offer some useful advice.*

FOLLOW IT UP

★ Have students extend this lesson in tact to real-life situations, as they arise.

Name: _____

⭐ WRITE AWAY!
We'll Call You

🔑 A *rejection* letter is a polite way to say no.

✏️ Use the letter shell to draft a rejection letter.

_____
_____
_____

Dear_____,

Thank you for your interest in _____
_____.

Unfortunately, we have decided _____
_____.

This is because_____
_____
_____.

Here are some suggestions that may help you in the future. _____
_____
_____.

Good luck!

Yours truly,

_____

And NOW—
Rework your letter so that it is clear, honest, and direct. Write it as if someone were sending it to you. Make is as gentle and effective as you can.

More Ideas for Expository Writing

❑ Explain what to do to soothe a cranky baby.

❑ Explain how to make a collage.

❑ Explain the rules of a card game you like.

❑ Explain how to surf the Internet.

❑ Explain different ways to sort buttons.

❑ Explain how to share a pizza among eight people.

❑ Explain how to open a jar that's stuck.

❑ Explain how your family celebrates a certain holiday.

❑ Explain how to tell fiction from nonfiction.

❑ Explain what to do to calm jittery nerves.

❑ Explain how to get information about a celebrity.

❑ Explain to a young child why it's important to brush teeth.

❑ Explain a trick you use to remember something.

❑ Explain what you do when you can't fall asleep.

❑ Explain what to do if you miss the school bus.

❑ Explain what makes people hiccup.

❑ Explain how a piano works.

❑ Explain how to blow a bubble with bubble gum.

❑ Explain what to do in a fire drill.

❑ Explain how to do a certain kind of dance.

❑ Explain why a good plan went wrong.

❑ Explain how to teach someone to ride a bike.

❑ Explain how your city or state got its name.

❑ Explain how to give a speech to a large audience.

❑ Explain how to play a musical instrument.

Write to Persuade

The goal of **persuasive** writing is to offer an opinion supported by facts. Persuasive writing attempts to convince the reader to agree with the author's point of view. Persuasive writing works best when facts and examples back up the author's statements.

Techniques of persuasive writing include the use of comparison and value words, such as *better, more precise,* or *safest.* Persuasive writing must be logical and convincing, but to be most effective it should not hit the reader over the head!

EVALUATION TIPS

There are many ways to evaluate students' persuasive writing. Here are some broad points to consider as you judge some or all of the writing activities in this section of the book:

Does the persuasive piece have—

❑ A clear audience and purpose?

❑ A logical plan of organization?

❑ A focused argument?

❑ Support through examples, logic, data, or other details?

❑ A strong conclusion?

❑ A reasonable and/or respectful tone?

❑ Is the piece complete?

❑ Does it allow readers to evaluate the writer's point of view?

❑ Does it show planning and follow-through?

❑ Is the word choice thoughtful, precise, and persuasive?

❑ How are the mechanics (grammar, usage, spelling, punctuation)?

In So Many Words

Students will attempt to write persuasive statements—limited to 25 words or less!

SET THE STAGE

★ Tell students that some contests ask for written responses to a statement like "Why We Recycle," "What Flag Day Means to Me," or "How to Stop People From Smoking." Often, the rules limit responses to "25 words or less" or the entry will be disqualified. Talk about the problems of this limitation.

★ Help students pick subjects to address in 25 words or less. Some suggestions include "What Makes Me Unique," "The Best Pet/Hobby/Song/Sport/etc.," "Why [Name] is My Idol," "The Best Way to Spend Saturday," "How to Solve [A Problem]," "Reasons for Having Laws about [Topic]," "The Tastiest Vegetable," "Why I'd Fly in Space," "Why Never to Serve [Food] for Lunch," and "The Most Annoying Noise."

★ Duplicate and distribute the word count form on page 77. Have students list their topics, issues, or questions, and then complete the form. The 25 boxes provide one space for each of the 25 permitted words.

★ Tie this activity to literature, social studies, science, math, art, or other curriculum areas of interest in your class. Pose a question or make a statement related to the chosen area. Have students focus their persuasive arguments on responding to the question.

GUIDE THE WAY

★ You may want to specify that all students respond to the same topic, issue, or question. Or, you may permit students to select their own for a wider range of arguments.

★ Suggest that students use scrap paper for early drafts of their pieces. (Or provide extra copies of page 77.) Encourage writers to revise and refine their writing until they are satisfied that the particular 25 words they've chosen give the best possible response.

★ Point out to students that even though the final product will be very short, it may take them several tries to get it right. Brief, concise writing takes real effort.

Clarity—This task makes you be brief, but you must also be very clear. Does your 25-words-or-less statement make its point clearly? Directly? Strongly?

FOLLOW IT UP

★ Challenge students to apply the 25-words-or-less limit to other kinds of writing.

Name: _____

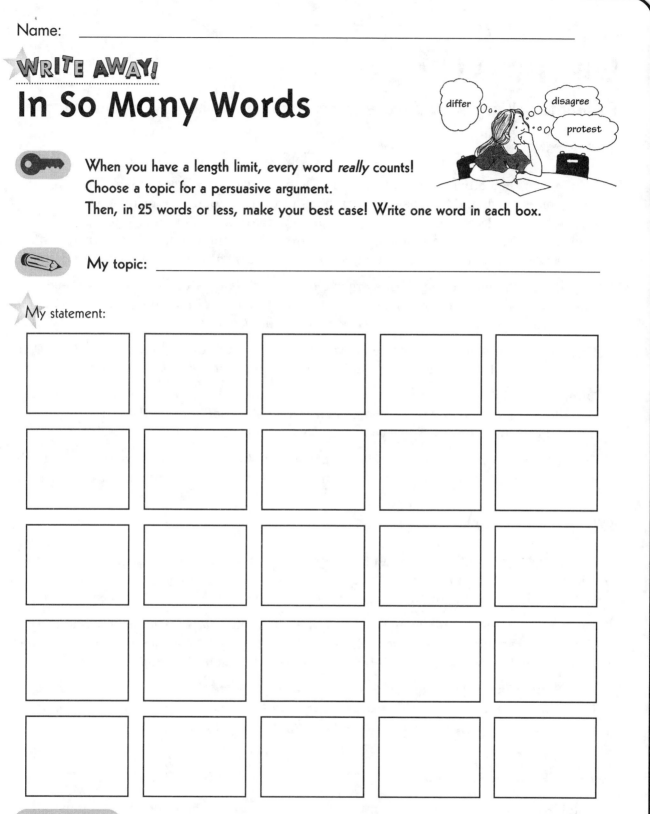

In So Many Words

differ

disagree

protest

🔑 When you have a length limit, every word *really* counts!
Choose a topic for a persuasive argument.
Then, in 25 words or less, make your best case! Write one word in each box.

✏️ My topic: _____

★ My statement:

And NOW—

Share your statement with others. Ask their opinions. Did you make a strong case? Did you convince them? Rework your 25 words to make your point more effectively.

Giving Advice

Dear Darryl,
I strongly advise
that you study
for Monday's final
exam.
John

Students will use their powers of persuasion to give advice to someone.

SET THE STAGE

★ People give each other advice all the time. Define *advice* as suggestions or ideas about what someone should do. Discuss situations in which people give or take advice. Examples include doctors advising patients how to treat an illness or injury; teachers advising students how to study for a test; parents advising children how to respond to an emergency; friends advising each other how to deal with certain social situations.

★ Discuss questions like these: *Has anyone ever asked you for advice? Have you ever given advice? Which do you prefer, giving advice or getting it? Who do you usually turn to for advice? What is the difference between giving advice and being bossy?*

★ Display examples of letters and responses that appear in advice columns, such as *Dear Abby, Ask Ann Landers,* or other similar features found in newspapers and magazines.

★ Duplicate and distribute the advice organizer on page 79. Students can use this to help them formulate good advice for someone in a real situation (or one that they have experienced themselves). Or they can advise someone about a fictional problem.

★ Students might write problems on slips of paper and put them into a box or envelope. Each student can then select a slip at random and compose a response that gives useful advice.

GUIDE THE WAY

★ It may help for students to role-play various social situations in which the best course of action is not obvious. They can pause after they have presented problems, talk about what they might do, and discuss the pros and cons of every suggestion.

★ Explain to students that giving advice can be a delicate matter. The person who gives the advice should be supportive, helpful, and convincing. The advice should be do-able and reasonable. A useful test of advice is: *Would you follow this advice yourself?*

Logic and Examples—*It's not easy to give advice! When you do, support your ideas with logic or with examples that explain why it makes sense. Good advice may not be easy to follow through on, but it should be easy to understand!*

FOLLOW IT UP

★ Establish a regular advice column that you display on a bulletin board or publish in a class newsletter. Students can take turns submitting questions and writing responses.

★ Extend by having students write advice to fictional characters or to historical figures. For example, they might write to the main character of a novel offering advice on how to deal with a problem that arises in the story. Or they might write to give George Washington advice on how to be a good president to a brand-new nation.

Name: _____

WRITE AWAY!
Giving Advice

Dear Darryl,
I strongly advise
that you study
for Monday's final
exam.
John

Advice is a suggestion or idea. Advice tells how to do something.
People seek advice to solve problems or to fix bad situations.
Here's a problem or bad situation: _____

_____

_____

Give some good advice. Persuade the person that your ideas are wise.

⭐ What the person should do: _____

_____

_____

_____

_____

⭐ What the person should *not* do: _____

_____

_____

_____

_____

⭐ A last bit of advice: _____

_____

_____

_____

And NOW—

Use the suggestions in a letter of advice. Explain why your ideas are good. Convince the person
that your advice can help. Be sure you'd be willing to follow your own advice!

Couch Critic

Students will write reviews of movies, videos, or television shows.

SET THE STAGE

★ Display written reviews of books, movies, videos, television shows, or concerts.

★ Explore the language of reviewing by clarifying words, such as *criticize, analyze, evaluate*, and *recommend*. Point out that although the word *criticize* has a negative connotation in daily speech, it has a different meaning in a review. A reviewer must be critical—must make an assessment or judgment—about a work to evaluate it. A critical review helps an audience know more about a work and may persuade them either to avoid a work or to give it a try.

★ Discuss questions like these: *Have you ever read a review that made you want to see a movie or TV show—or made you want to skip it? Are reviews all positive or negative? What should reviews tell? What should they not tell? Everyone is entitled to an opinion, so how can one person's review help others?*

★ Duplicate and distribute the reviewer's plan on page 81. Students can use it to gather details for a critical review.

★ Students might draft individual reviews of the same video or TV show, and then collaborate on a single review that gives the best points, both positive and negative.

GUIDE THE WAY

★ Help students develop useful criteria for a critical review. For example, they must go beyond summarizing plot, identifying characters, or simply saying whether or not they liked the show. They might analyze its theme, evaluate the script or acting, comment on how effective (realistic, funny, engaging, scary, etc.) the work is, and so on.

★ Reassure students that a review can be *both* positive and negative. Most works have good and bad points. Students should keep this in mind as they formulate their ideas.

Purpose—*Before you criticize any work, take time to think about it. Form your own opinions. Do you want to persuade people to see the show? Do you want to steer them away from it? Do you want to recommend it only to certain viewers? Do you want to highlight its strong aspects, discuss its flaws, or both? Let your goals guide you.*

FOLLOW IT UP

★ Have students share their reviews orally or by posting them in a reviewer's notebook.

★ Extend by having students write reviews of other kinds of experiences. They might critique a new bookstore, a playground, a museum, a party, or a sports team.

Name: _____

WRITE AWAY!
Couch Critic

🔑 A *critic* reviews works. The review gives the writer's opinions. A review can be positive, negative, or both.

✏️ Pick a movie, video, or television show to review. Answer the questions to help you plan your review.

⭐ Title: _____

⭐ Setting: _____

⭐ Main character(s): _____

_____

⭐ Main idea: _____

_____

⭐ Strengths: _____

_____

_____

_____

⭐ Weaknesses: _____

_____

_____

_____

⭐ Who should see it? _____

And NOW—

Use the details above to write your review. Make it interesting to read, even to those who don't know the show. Persuade your audience: Should they see it or skip it?

Take Out an Ad

Students will create written advertisements.

Exercise Is BEAR-y Good For You!

SET THE STAGE

★ Display an assortment of print ads for various products that interest students such as toys, books, clothing, sports gear, music, or movies. Select a variety of ads. Point out the *slogan*—a phrase or motto that expresses a goal or belief.

★ Make a videotape of some TV commercials. Watch them with students. Guide them in analyzing the words and techniques that persuade people to take interest in the products.

★ Discuss questions like these: *How does an advertisement use words to persuade or convince? How does the information given in an ad affect the decisions you make about that product? What catches an audience's attention in an ad?*

★ Duplicate and distribute the ad planner on page 83. Challenge students to use this organizer to plan an ad that will convince people to take interest in a product.

★ Students might design or invent new products and then create written ads for the products. Or they can create ads for existing products or to support a good cause.

GUIDE THE WAY

★ If necessary, help students pick the products to advertise. It may be easiest for them to focus on products they use or like. However, it can be an interesting challenge for students to write effective ads for products that they neither use nor endorse!

★ Emphasize three kinds of supporting details that can make an advertisement effective. Students can include *facts* (truthful statements), *statistics* or *data* (facts based on numbers), and *quotations* (exact words that other people have said).

★ Some ads grab attention by using exaggeration, questions, surprising facts, humor, drama, mystery, or some combination of these elements. Guide students to use whatever strategies they think work best.

> **Evidence!**—*The best way to persuade an audience is to support what you say. You can use facts, logic, data, or quotations. It's fine to include opinions, too. But try to give some facts that speak for themselves.*

FOLLOW IT UP

★ Have students display their ads on a bulletin board. Discuss the different strategies ad writers used to get their messages across.

★ Extend by having students prepare scripts for commercials, based on the written ads. Students can envision (and perform!) the commercials as radio or television spots.

Name: _____

WRITE AWAY!
Take Out an Ad

Exercise Is
BEAR-y
Good For
You!

🔑 An *ad* (short for *advertisement*) is a message meant to persuade.

✏️ Pick a product to advertise. Use this form to plan how to interest people in it.

⭐ Name of product: _____

⭐ What it is: _____

⭐ Its best features: _____

_____

_____

⭐ Audience: _____

⭐ How to grab attention: _____

_____

⭐ Facts: _____

_____

⭐ Data: _____

_____

⭐ Quotations: _____

_____

⭐ Clever ending: _____

_____

And NOW—

Use your notes to write the actual ad, known as the *copy*. Think about your audience. Use a jazzy introduction. And don't forget a catchy *slogan*, or tag line.

To a "T"

Students will create brief persuasive messages that might appear on T-shirts.

SET THE STAGE ★

★ Display an assortment of bumper stickers, campaign buttons, or advertising slogans with persuasive message.

★ Look around the classroom to see if anyone is wearing a T-shirt that displays a message. Talk about the message, how it is conveyed, and how it might be improved or edited.

★ Discuss questions like these: *Why do you think that T-shirts are popular for displaying messages? What do T-shirt messages have in common? What kinds of messages don't make sense appearing on T-shirts?*

★ Duplicate and distribute the T-shirt outline on page 85.

★ Students might consider a two-sided (front-and-back) T-shirt message. On the front, they might ask a question or present a statement that captures attention. On the back, they can respond persuasively. In that case, give students two copies of page 85.

GUIDE THE WAY ★

★ Help students focus their persuasive messages so that they are brief and catchy.

★ Invite students to use an interesting, but legible, print style and particular colors or designs that will enhance the message.

> **Purpose**—*The goal of persuasion is to get people to do what you want, or think as you do. Does your T-shirt message make its point? How can you jazz it up? Would you be proud to wear the T-shirt yourself?*

FOLLOW IT UP ★

★ Have students use fabric paints or crayons to put their messages on real T-shirts.

★ Work with the art teacher on a project to create class or school T-shirts that convey a persuasive message.

Name: _____

⭐ WRITE AWAY!
To a "T"

🔑 T-shirts can be great places for sharing messages.
Think of a message you'd like people to notice.
Think of how to say it briefly, cleverly, persuasively,
and with pizzazz!

✏️ Design a T-shirt that carries your message.

And NOW—

Create an ad for your T-shirt. Persuade people to wear it.

Inviting Invitations

Students will write letters of invitation to persuade birds to stop by for snacks!

Try Our Delicious Snacks!

SET THE STAGE

★ Display an assortment of different invitations. Guide students to identify the key elements including occasion/event, host, date and time, place, and what to wear or bring.

★ Discuss questions like these: *Have you ever been invited to something other than a party? What kind of event was it? What about invitations gets your interest? What persuades you to accept or refuse the invitation? If you were unsure, what kind of information would you want to have?*

★ Tell students that in this activity, they will write an inviting letter to a bird, persuading it to stop at the writer's bird feeder, or build a nest in the writer's yard.

★ Duplicate and distribute the invitation form on page 87. Point out that students need not complete the entire page to prepare for their invitations. Encourage them to develop the ideas they like best and can present most convincingly.

★ Students might wish to create their own twist on this activity. Alternate ideas might include inviting a stray animal to join the family; inviting a caterpillar to build its cocoon in a certain spot; inviting an owl to watch over your barn, and so on.

GUIDE THE WAY

★ The main task in this activity is to focus on the audience—in this case, a bird! Help students imagine what features would appeal to birds, so they can make the invitations all the more inviting.

★ To persuade the birds to accept the invitations, students must make the events sound too good to pass up. They can do this by including specific details about the bird feeders, nesting opportunities, shelter, water, safety, and so on.

Cause and Effect—One way to persuade is to show cause-and-effect relationships. You can do this by writing If . . . then . . . statements; for example: If you get tired of looking all over for food, then you might like to visit my bird feeder!

FOLLOW IT UP

★ Have students present their inviting invitations orally, in the form of a speech. They can deliver them in person or on tape.

★ As an extension, have students exchange invitations and write letters of acceptance (or refusal) from the points of view of the birds. Encourage them to give their reasons for accepting and what they especially look forward to. If they choose to turn down the invitations, they should specify those reasons.

Name: _____

Try Our Delicious Snacks!

WRITE AWAY!
Inviting Invitations

 Invitations ask you to go somewhere or take part in something.
Use your imagination to write an invitation—to a bird! Ask it to stop for a meal at your bird feeder. Or invite it to build a nest in a tree near your home.

✎ Use this table to collect ideas for your letter of invitation.

What Birds Want	What I Can Offer

And NOW—

Use the ideas you gathered to write a letter of invitation to the bird.
Make your offer sound too good to pass up! Include convincing details.

Dear Editor

Students will write letters to editors.

SET THE STAGE

★ Explain that an editorial is a brief opinion piece published in a magazine or newspaper. An editorial states the point of view that the editors of the magazine or paper hold. Editorials invite people to write letters to respond. Many such letters are printed to show the give-and-take that the publication inspires in its readers.

★ Display examples of letters written to the editor of magazines or newspapers.

★ Help students recognize elements that all the letters share: they offer a reader's opinion on or response to something published in the magazine or paper. Most letters briefly refer to the article in question. They go on to give the writer's own views in an effort to persuade other readers to agree.

★ Discuss questions like these: *Have you ever read an article that made you want to respond? What kinds of things would you want to tell the editors? Do you think editors like to get letters from their readers? Why?*

★ Duplicate and distribute the letter organizer on page 89.

★ You may want students to respond to the same article. Or you might have pairs read articles, discuss them, and draft joint letters to the editor that summarizes their responses.

GUIDE THE WAY

★ Direct students to articles that spark debate. For instance, they'd probably have many things to say in response to articles that call for year-round school, an end to recycling, or penalties for not wearing bike helmets.

★ Help students organize supporting details for their letters. If they agree with the ideas in the articles, they can list reasons for their support and praise the editors for bringing the subjects to people's attention. To disagree, they can give point-by-point counter-arguments and offer advice, opinions, or solutions of their own.

> **That's an Order!**—*Help readers follow your arguments. Set apart your points. Try using words like* first, second, third, *and* finally.

FOLLOW IT UP

★ Have students send their letters to the editors of the articles to which they responded.

★ Set up an ongoing current events interactive bulletin board. Post a timely article from a newspaper or magazine. Invite students to write brief responses in favor of or in opposition to it.

WRITE AWAY!
Dear Editor

🔑 Write to the editor to respond to something you read in a magazine or newspaper. You can agree or disagree with an article, but be clear about your reasons.

✏️ Use this organizer to plan a letter to an editor.

⭐ Name of article: _____

⭐ Where you read it: _____

⭐ Main idea(s) of the article: _____
_____
_____

⭐ What you agree with: _____
_____

⭐ What you disagree with: _____
_____

⭐ Supporting details to include: _____
_____
_____
_____
_____

And NOW—

Write the letter to the editor. Refer to the article. Politely tell why you agree or disagree with it. Give facts, quotations, data, or other evidence to support your ideas.

Billboards

Students will **create catchy slogans or other brief statement to make people take notice!**

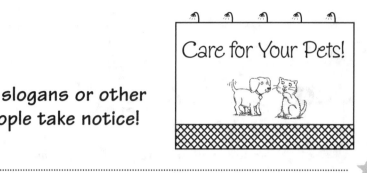

SET THE STAGE

★ Explain that a *billboard* is a large outdoor sign that displays ads, slogans, or public service announcements. Because they are meant to be seen from afar, often as people travel past them, they can't have too many words; the words they do have must be clear and easy to read.

★ Talk about billboards students have seen in your area. You might ask them to note the billboards they pass on their way to or from school.

★ Discuss questions like these: *Why do people or businesses pay to have their messages displayed on billboards? How do billboards get ideas across? Some people believe that billboards are "pollution for the eyes." Do you agree or disagree?*

★ Have students pick points to get across to others through billboards. They can work individually or in pairs. The billboard can include words *and* visuals.

★ Duplicate and distribute the billboard builder on page 91.

★ As a variation on this activity, have students identify existing billboards and write persuasive responses.

GUIDE THE WAY

★ Most billboards rely on color, design, and visual images to support the words and the message. Invite students to consider these elements as they create their own.

★ Help students think of messages they would like to convey. The message might be a public service statement (recycle cans and bottles, care for your pet, etc.), a plea for health or safety (brush your teeth, wear seatbelts, avoid drugs, etc.), a political idea (vote for —-, support —-, etc.), or a straightforward advertisement.

> **Sum It Up**—*Think of a billboard as a big summary of a big idea. Think about the main idea you want to get across. Pick your words carefully. Then figure out ways to make your message "pop"!*

FOLLOW IT UP

★ Have students create billboards on a classroom wall. The message can change weekly. Assign a different student or group to be responsible for a new billboard each week.

★ Invite someone who works for an outdoor advertising company to address the class. They can explain how billboards are made, put up, maintained, and changed. Students can write letters of invitation, and prepare written questions in advance.

Name: _____

WRITE AWAY!
Billboards

Care for Your Pets!

🔑 A *billboard* is a large outdoor sign used to display a message. Think of a message you'd like to share with lots of people.

✏️ List some ideas here. _____

_____

_____

Now design a billboard for your best idea. Make it eye-catching.

And NOW—

Write a letter to tell why you think your billboard should appear in a public space. Be persuasive! Tell who would see the billboard, how it can help, and why it's important.

Write to Make It Right

Students will write formal letters of complaint.

★ In a *letter of complaint*, a person writes to a business to register a formal protest. Most letters of complaint end with a request for the business to fix a problem, replace faulty merchandise, offer a refund, or right a wrong.

★ Brainstorm reasons why young people might write letters of complaint. Examples include writing to a toy company about a toy that broke too easily; a game manufacturer about missing pieces; or a store about poor service or lack of merchandise.

★ Discuss questions like these: *Have you ever wanted to complain about something, but you weren't sure how, or to whom? How can you decide whether a problem is big enough for a formal written complaint? How can you make a company listen to you?*

★ Duplicate and distribute the complaint chart on page 93.

★ Have students write a group letter of complaint about an issue that concerns the class, such as errors in textbooks, hard-to-use software, bad lunch menus, or high movie prices.

★ Put a humorous spin on the activity by having students imagine funny or exasperating problems. Examples include the following: *There are flies in my fries! There are no words on the last page of a mystery story! The store ran out of candles on my birthday!*

GUIDE THE WAY

★ Highlight the two main goals of any letter of complaint—to identify and explain a problem, and then to propose a reasonable solution that will satisfy.

★ Remind students that although a letter of complaint has a negative message to convey, it should be written in a positive, formal way. Tell students that to get results, they should be polite, write clearly, and provide enough details so the reader can sympathize with the problem and be motivated to help.

> ***Don't Whine, Shine!***— *A letter of complaint is about a problem or disappointment. But it shouldn't sound whiny or shrill. It should sound clear, with details to back up the complaint. No insults! State what you want to have happen. Do you want your money back? Do you want a replacement? Do you want an apology? Make a request that fits the problem, and you may get the results you want!*

FOLLOW IT UP

★ Have students keep copies of their letters, mail the originals, and await responses. As responses arrive, have students revisit the originals to see how requests were met.

Name: _____

Write to Make It Right

 A *letter of complaint* describes a problem and tries to persuades someone to set it right.

✏️ Plan a letter of complaint. Use this table to organize your ideas.

The Problem	
What Happened	
When It Happened	
How or Why It Happened	
How It Has Affected You	
What You Want Done	

And NOW—

Use the details from the table to write the formal letter of complaint. Be truthful and reasonable. Stay polite, businesslike, but firm. Persuade the reader to do what you ask.

My Fellow Americans

Students will write political speeches.

SET THE STAGE

★ Display pictures of famous leaders, such as presidents, members of Congress, monarchs, or civil rights leaders. Define *politics* as the science or art of government. Politics affects elections, laws, court decisions, government policies, and other areas of citizen's lives.

★ Explain that politicians give many speeches, and that speeches are a key part of the political process.

★ Read or play an audiocassette of Dr. Martin Luther King, Jr.'s stirring "I Have a Dream" speech.

★ Discuss questions like these: *Have you ever given a speech in front of a group? Have you ever listened to a speech? What were these experiences like? What political issues interest you? Why do they interest you? What makes speech writing different from other kinds of writing?*

★ Duplicate and distribute the cluster map on page 95. Have students use it to help them plan a speech that they might give to the class.

★ If politics seems too remote for your students, suggest that they write speeches about something of concern to the class, school, community, or to people their age.

GUIDE THE WAY

★ Tell students that speech writing is persuasive writing. The object is to make points to get across in spoken form. A speech needs an introduction, a body, and a conclusion.

★ Suggest that students drive home their main points with repetition. They might think of great phrases, then repeat the phrases occasionally to emphasize the point. Or they might repeat how they begin or end sentences. Caution them not to overuse this strategy.

★ Abraham Lincoln, one of America's greatest speakers, often used a "folksy" style in his speeches. Tell students that a speech can include jokes, personal anecdotes, or other light touches to engage listeners, as long as they fit the main point of the speech.

Sound Devices—*Speeches may sound better if they include a sound device, such as alliteration. Alliteration is the repeating of initial sounds, like **p**ollution **p**oisons **P**eoria, or **s**tudents **s**tand **s**trong. But don't overdo it.*

FOLLOW IT UP

★ Have students deliver their speeches to the class or to smaller groups.

★ As an extension, challenge students to prepare speeches as a fresh way to present their next book reports. Invite them to read quotations from the works, or provide background about the authors, the themes of the book, or anything else about the books.

WRITE AWAY!
My Fellow Americans

🔑 A *speech* is a talk given to a group of people. Speeches are given orally, but usually are written out beforehand. Speakers also practice their speeches to get ready.

✏️ Pick a political topic that interests you. Imagine giving a speech on it. Convince people to agree with your ideas. Use the cluster map to gather ideas for your speech.

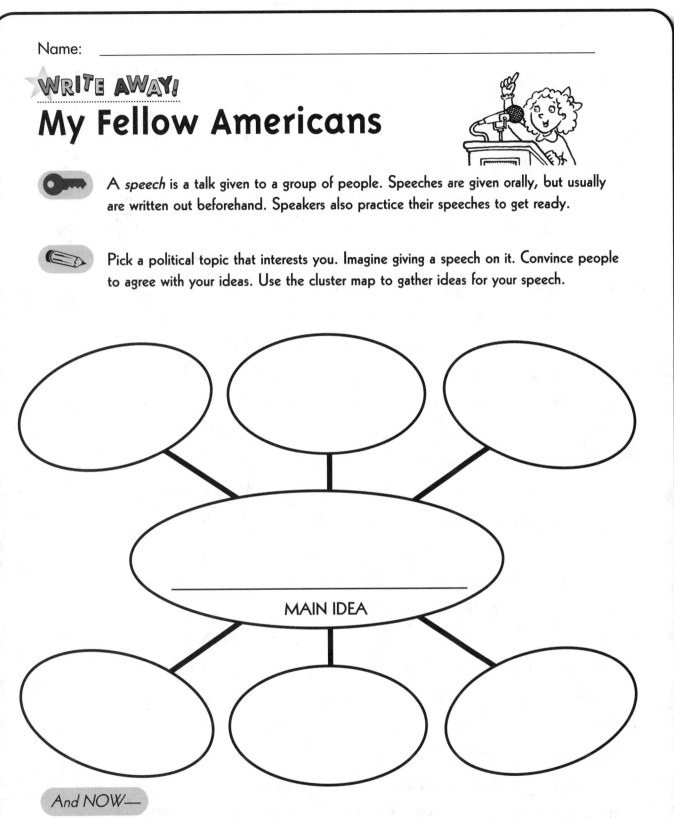

MAIN IDEA

And NOW—

Use your best points in a speech to your class. State your main idea near the start. Include details that support your ideas. You can add other points to interest your audience. Use a style that appeals to you. Practice your speech in front of a mirror.

More Ideas for Persuasive Writing

❑ Write a piece to convince your parents to let you have a pet.

❑ Write a piece to convince your teacher not to assign homework.

❑ Write a piece to convince a neighbor to feed your cat.

❑ Write a piece to convince lawmakers to make your birthday an official holiday.

❑ Write a piece to convince someone to hire you as a helper.

❑ Write a piece to convince people to learn a certain song.

❑ Write a piece to convince someone to explore a cave with you.

❑ Write a piece to convince someone to buy a certain car.

❑ Write a piece to convince someone to support your favorite team.

❑ Write a piece to convince the principal that [name] is the best teacher in school.

❑ Write a piece to convince your parents to raise your allowance.

❑ Write a piece to convince NASA to choose you to be an astronaut.

❑ Write a piece to convince a judge to pick your work for the art show.

❑ Write a piece to convince people to ride bicycles to work.

❑ Write a piece to convince a store to carry a certain item.

❑ Write a piece to convince a factory to stop polluting.

❑ Write a piece to convince people to wear sunscreen.

❑ Write a piece to convince shoppers to come to a certain store.

❑ Write a piece to convince people to give up watching television for a week.

❑ Write a piece to convince your family to take a vacation in New York City.

❑ Write a piece to convince people to take part in a walk-a-thon.

❑ Write a piece to convince a friend to trust you.

❑ Write a piece to convince the coach to let girls play on the football team.

❑ Write a piece to convince your teacher to get a particular class pet.

The Big Book of Ready-to-Go Writing Lessons • Scholastic Professional Books

Write in the Real World

The goal of **practical** writing is to respond in writing to real-world situations. Practical writing includes writing to deliver messages, fill out forms, make requests, or establish lines of communication. Real-world writing works best when it is concise, clear, and to the point.

Techniques of practical writing include the use of facts and details, lists, charts, diagrams, or other precise data. Practical writing should conform to any given rules or guidelines; it should be accessible to a wide audience.

EVALUATION TIPS

There are many ways to evaluate students' real-world writing. Here are some broad points to consider as you judge some or all of the writing activities in this section of the book:

Does the practical piece have—

❑ A clear purpose or focus?

❑ A sensible plan of organization?

❑ A solution to a problem?

❑ Suitable language and tone?

❑ Any extra or confusing information?

❑ Is the piece complete?

❑ Does it meet its intended purpose?

❑ Does it show planning and follow-through?

❑ Is the word choice thoughtful, precise, and appropriate?

❑ How are the mechanics (grammar, usage, spelling, punctuation)?

May I Take a Message?

Students will write detailed telephone messages, based on role-played phone calls.

SET THE STAGE

★ Talk about the importance of leaving an accurate telephone message for someone. Invite students to give examples of messages they have taken. Some might be willing to describe what happened when they forgot to relay messages or mixed up the details.

★ Discuss questions like these: *Have you ever taken a phone message? What important details did you have to remember? How did you remind yourself of these details? Has anyone ever left a telephone message for you? What did you want to know?*

★ Duplicate and distribute the While You Were Out form on page 99.

★ Students might take copies of the form home and use it in real-life family situations.

GUIDE THE WAY

★ Divide the class into pairs or small groups. Invite them to role-play telephone calls in which someone leaves information for someone who isn't there. The person who takes the message must figure out how to leave the important details for the absent person.

★ Possible subjects include an invitation to a party, the need to cancel an existing plan, a call from the family dentist about an appointment, or a message from a friend about tonight's homework.

★ After the role-playing, have students work together to formulate reasonable written messages to leave for whomever wasn't there to receive the calls.

★ Explain that someone who takes a message for another person has a responsibility to get the main details. It's the key to helping the person respond appropriately.

> **Be Reliable**—*You don't have to write a phone message in full sentences. Fragments and phrases are okay. But you must be clear about the name of the person who called, the phone number, the time of the call, and what the absent person is expected to do. What if it were a message for you? You'd want all the details, wouldn't you?*

FOLLOW IT UP

★ Have students create their own telephone message forms.

★ Challenge students to keep telephone logs of the calls they make and receive over the course of a week. Then have them write brief reports about the way they spend their telephone time based on this data.

Name: _____

WRITE AWAY!
May I Take a Message?

🔑 Many people today have answering machines and voice mail.
But it's still important to know how to take a telephone message in writing.

✏️ Role-play a phone call for someone who isn't home. Take a message for the person.
Help him or her know how to return the call or act on the message. Use this form.

WHILE YOU WERE OUT

Date _____ Time _____

Name _____

Phone number _____

❑ Called	❑ Will call back
❑ Returned your call	❑ Wants you to call back

Message _____

_____

_____

_____

_____

_____

_____

_____

Message taken by _____

And NOW—

Use the details in the phone message. Summarize them in a paragraph.

Greetings!

Students will create original greeting cards.

SET THE STAGE

★ Display an assortment of greeting cards that express wishes for birthdays, holidays, and anniversaries. Also include get well, thank you, bon voyage, and congratulations cards.

★ Discuss questions like these: *Why do people send greeting cards? Have you ever picked out a greeting card for someone? What do you look for in a greeting card? Do you like funny cards, serious cards, mushy cards, or plain cards? Which do you prefer to get?*

★ Duplicate and distribute the greeting card planner on page 101.

★ Students might write poems that suit the chosen occasions.

GUIDE THE WAY

★ Help students decide which occasion they wish to commemorate in a greeting card. Allow them to select the type of card or assign one to them.

★ After students plan the words that will appear on the cards, encourage them to make cards out of construction paper. They can add artistic touches, such as glitter, lace, pinked edges, ribbon, or pictures cut from magazines.

> *From the Heart*—*People spend billions of dollars on store-bought greeting cards, but nothing beats a card with a personal touch. Put a little of yourself in the message. Customize it for the person the card is for. You can make it funny, sweet, poetic, or serious. Use colors, designs, and pictures you know the person likes.*

FOLLOW IT UP

★ Have students display their cards or send them.

★ Invite students to create cards for actual occasions: Mother's Day, Flag Day, and so on.

Name: _____

WRITE AWAY!
Greetings!

🔑 You can send greeting cards for any occasion.
You can express almost any message.

✏️ Pick a reason to send a card to someone.

- ❏ Happy Birthday
- ❏ Happy Holiday
- ❏ Happy Anniversary

- ❏ Get Well
- ❏ I'm Sorry
- ❏ Thank You

- ❏ Congratulations
- ❏ Bon Voyage
- ❏ Other _____

Who is the card for? _____

What theme will the card feature? _____

Pick a tone.

- ❏ Funny
- ❏ Serious

- ❏ Sweet
- ❏ Mushy

- ❏ Plain
- ❏ Other _____

Pick a card style.

- ❏ Standard (left fold)

- ❏ Vertical (top fold)

- ❏ Pop-Up

- ❏ Window

- ❏ Accordion

- ❏ Other _____

And NOW—

Design and create a greeting card. Use words and phrases that express how you feel. Use construction paper to make the card. Decorate it as you like. Make the card fit the person—and make it clear that it's from you.

Fan Mail

Students will write fan letters to famous people or characters.

SET THE STAGE

★ Tell students that a *fan* is someone who is very interested in or enthusiastic about something or someone. Students may be sports fans, music fans, dance fans, pizza fans, and so on. A *fan letter* is a letter a fan writes to someone he or she admires.

★ Discuss questions like these: *Have you ever wanted to write to a famous person? What would you say to the person? What would you like to find out? What would you tell about yourself? Would you make any special requests? How do you think it feels to receive a fan letter?*

★ Brainstorm with the class to list famous people they might want to contact.

★ Duplicate and distribute the fan mail planner on page 103. Students can use this to scope out their letter.

★ Students might write fan letters to themselves, which reflect what they would like to have someone say about them.

GUIDE THE WAY

★ Point out that most fans are strangers to the people they write to. Therefore, writers of fan letters must introduce themselves and tell how they came to be fans.

★ A fan letter can request something special, such as a reply, an autographed photo, a team picture, or other token that a famous person would be willing to share.

> **Set the Scene**—*You may know quite a bit about some celebrities. But remember, you are a stranger to them. Break the ice by telling a little bit about yourself: who you are, where you live, and how you came to be a fan. Make yourself come alive to the reader, so he or she will want to reply to you.*

FOLLOW IT UP

★ Invite students to share their letters in small groups. Then, have them mail the letters to the people they wrote to.

★ Take a cross-curricular slant by asking students to compose fan letters to favorite historical figures, scientists, explorers, inventors, or fictional characters.

Name: _____

★WRITE AWAY!
Fan Mail

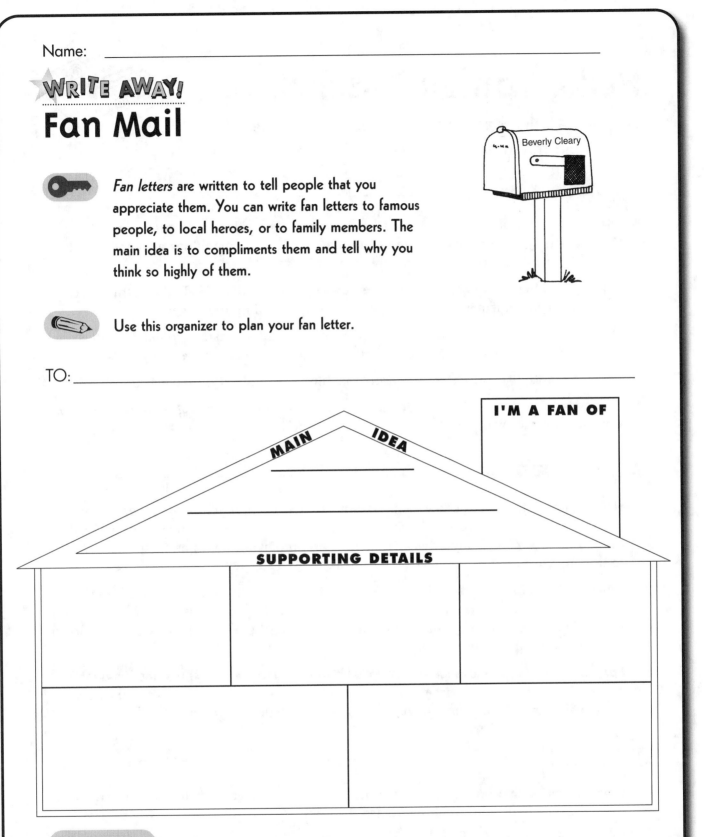

Fan letters are written to tell people that you appreciate them. You can write fan letters to famous people, to local heroes, or to family members. The main idea is to compliments them and tell why you think so highly of them.

Use this organizer to plan your fan letter.

TO: _____

I'M A FAN OF

MAIN   IDEA
_____

_____

SUPPORTING DETAILS

And NOW—

Use the ideas above to write a fantastic fan letter. Begin by telling who you are and why you're a fan. Then pay your compliments. Tell why you think the person is so special. End with a request, if you have one. Or restate how terrific you think that person is.

Hello, You've Reached . . .

Students will create messages for telephone answering machines.

★ Discuss why people have answering machines. Invite students to share some of the messages they have heard. Students who have answering machines at home might share the messages their machines play for callers.

★ Play some different answering machine messages, if possible. Talk about the safety issues involved in leaving a useful but not overly revealing message.

★ Discuss questions like these: *What information should an answering machine message include? What should it NOT give? What can a message include besides words?*

★ Duplicate and distribute the answering machine script sheet on page 105.

★ Students might include "stage directions" for recording the messages so that they convey the tone they want.

⭐ GUIDE THE WAY

★ Help students identify the key elements for an answering machine message: what number the caller has reached, whose phone it is, how to leave a message, how long a message to leave, and any other details that are important (such as to speak slowly or to include your area code.)

★ After students have written out their scripts, have them check that the messages say what they want to say. Invite students to practice saying the messages until they think the messages sound smooth and natural. Encourage them to edit the words to encourage callers to want to leave messages.

> **Length Counts**—*A message on an answering machine should be just long enough to include key details. If you aren't there, there's no need to tie up the caller any longer than necessary. Make your message, short, sweet, clear, and direct.*

⭐ FOLLOW IT UP

★ Have students tape-record the answering machine messages. Invite them to play back the messages to decide which messages they like.

★ Extend the activity by having students create possible answering machine messages for famous people, for stores or businesses, or for a school or other institution.

Name: _____

⭐ WRITE AWAY!
Hello, You've Reached . . .

 An answering machine takes messages when you can't get to the phone yourself.

Imagine that you have a new answering machine. Write a cheerful, useful greeting. Invite callers to leave a message for you. Tell them what details to include.

_____
_____
_____
_____
_____
_____
_____
_____
_____
_____
_____

And NOW—

Share your message with a friend. Ask for comments: Is the message clear? Is it complete? Is it polite? Should you add anything else?

Find the Way

Students will write sets of directions for friends to follow.

SET THE STAGE

★ Discuss the various ways people give directions. For instance, they use maps, mention landmarks, estimate travel times or distances, and so on.

★ Discuss questions like these: *Have you ever told someone how to get to your school? What was that experience like? What do you have to know before you can give good directions? Is there sometimes more than one way to get to a place? If so, which way would you describe, and why? Are the directions easy or hard? What landmarks or details would you include?*

★ Duplicate and distribute the directions organizer on page 107.

★ Students might draw maps to accompany their written directions.

★ As an alternative, students might give directions from school to another destination: a mall, a park, a museum, a historical spot, a local landmark, and so on.

GUIDE THE WAY

★ Remind students to use direction words, such as *left, right, straight, north, south, east, west, uptown, downtown,* and so on. Suggest that they include street names, landmarks, estimated distances or times, and any other visual clues that can help.

★ It's smart to include the school's telephone number with the directions. That way, if the person gets lost, he or she can call to the destination for more help.

Order Counts!—When you give directions, they must be in order. A good way to check is to follow the directions yourself, exactly as written. Be sure that they work!

FOLLOW IT UP

★ Have students try to follow each other's directions.

★ As an extension, have students create a class atlas, comprised of maps from the school to various locations in the community.

Name: _____

WRITE AWAY!
Find The Way

🔑 *Directions* tell how to get from one place to another. People need good directions whether they drive, walk, ride a bike, take a bus, or travel any other way.

✏️ Plan a set of directions to your school. (If you need more space, use the back.)

School Address: _____

School Telephone Number: _____

How to get there from _____ :

1. _____

   _____

2. _____

   _____

3. _____

   _____

4. _____

   _____

5. _____

   _____

And NOW—

Go over the directions, step by step. Did you clearly tell what to do? Did you use direction words, like *left, right, straight, and continue?* Check that you've given all the key details. Then make a simple map to go with your directions.

In an Emergency

Students will write brief scripts to help them role-play imaginary 911 calls.

SET THE STAGE

★ Emphasize that a call to 911 should *only* be made in the case of a true emergency—one that requires immediate police, fire department, or medical attention. Discuss the serious repercussions of abusing the 911 service through frivolous use.

★ Talk with students about the importance of presenting crucial information in a clear way when communicating with a 911 operator. Time is essential in most 911 situations, so a caller must be calm, direct, and concise. Inform students that most 911 operators have the training and experience to ask questions to get the data they need to send help.

★ Discuss questions like these: *What constitutes a true emergency? Who might you contact for less critical problems? What information should you be ready to give to the 911 operator? What information is unnecessary? Why is it important to stay calm?*

★ Discuss operator questions like these: *What do you need to find out? What would you say to calm someone who is frightened? What if you didn't know what to do yourself?*

★ Duplicate and distribute the 911 script planner on page 109.

★ Invite an emergency worker to address the class on this important topic.

GUIDE THE WAY

★ Give groups of students time to brainstorm a legitimate emergency situation.

★ Guide students to envision a situation in which they alone would responsible for making a 911 call—i.e., there is no adult present to take charge, or it's clear that immediate help is necessary.

★ Within groups, one person (or pair) acts as the caller, another as the 911 operator. Other students can act as moderators, to prompt or guide the role-players if they miss any important points. Have students talk together about what they would ask if they were the 911 operator and what they would say as the caller.

Get It Clear!—*This kind of writing can be creative, but it must be accurate. It matters that you select and present the key details accurately, clearly, and briefly.*

FOLLOW IT UP

★ Invite students to present their 911 role-plays for classmates. Or tape-record the "calls" so others can hear and critique them.

★ After students have had the experience role-playing 911 calls, see how they respond as callers and 911 operators to a hypothetical emergency that you present to them.

Name: _____

⭐ WRITE AWAY!
In an Emergency

 An *emergency* is a sudden, dangerous situation to deal with quickly. In most areas, you can dial 911 to report an emergency and ask for help. Imagine a situation that would prompt a call to 911. What would you say? How would the 911 operator respond?

✏️ Complete the script planner. Use it to help you role-play your imaginary 911 call.

Emergency: _____

911 Operator	Emergency Caller
Hello, this is 911.	

And NOW—

Role-play your imaginary 911 call for your classmates.

Want Ad

Students will write classified ads.

SET THE STAGE

★ Display classified ads from local newspapers. Highlight the categories that students might use in this activity including For Sale, Wanted to Buy, and Help Wanted. Invite students to read some of the ads to familiarize themselves with standard abbreviations, order, length, and other conventions.

★ Discuss how and why people place and use classified ads. Explain that most newspapers provide space for the ads as a way to raise money. Classified ads cost less than commercial ads. Readers may buy the newspaper specifically to get them.

★ Discuss questions like these: *Have you ever read the want ads? Which kinds of ads appeal to you? Have you ever placed an ad? How did you do it? What happened?*

★ Duplicate and distribute the want ad form on page 111. Help students understand how to use the form. Explain that each box will hold one letter, space, or punctuation mark. The shaded boxes mark the end of a line, when the ad is typeset as it will appear in the newspaper. Students need not use all four lines completely.

★ Rather than writing ads for items to buy or sell, or for jobs they could do, some students might write ads about their homes! In this fictional task, they could describe their homes as they might in classified ads for rental or sales property.

GUIDE THE WAY

★ Help students understand that most classified ads are brief, because their cost is determined by length. The writer of the ad must decide what key details to include to grab a reader's attention. The ad must be worded to be both truthful and appealing.

★ Have students write several versions of the ads and show them to classmates. Any questions or comments that arise can help the writers fine-tune the ads for clarity and effectiveness.

> **Connotation**—*Words are loaded with meaning beyond dictionary definitions. Which would you prefer—an* unwanted *bicycle or an* outgrown *bicycle? Which sounds better—a* shabby *chair or a* well-worn *one? Pick your words carefully. Think about what each word means. Imagine what readers will picture when they read.*

FOLLOW IT UP

★ Have students role-play conversations between potential buyers and sellers, or between potential employers and employees, based on the ads.

★ As a cross-curricular connection, challenge students to create mock want ads for famous inventions, cures, buildings, vehicles, bridges, and so on.

110

Name: _____

Want Ad

 A *want ad* is a short "blurb" printed in the back of a newspaper. It describes items that people hope to sell, rent, or buy, or jobs they want to fill or do for others. Most want ads are short because you pay by the word. Space is limited.

✏️ Use this form to create a want ad up to 4 lines long. (Each line ends at a black box.) Each line can have 35 letters and spaces—1 per box. (Each punctuation mark counts as 1 space.) Do NOT use abbreviations. Make your ad catchy but clear.

⭐ Name _____

⭐ Date _____

⭐ Type of Ad _____

And NOW—

Check for spelling, spaces between words, and punctuation. Then share your ad with two classmates. Use their suggestions to help you improve it.

Ask an Author

Students will write to authors.

★ SET THE STAGE

★ Display books your class has enjoyed. Include a variety of genres and authors.

★ Tell students that authors often discuss some of the key ideas that inspired them to write, or to create certain characters, settings, or plots. Examples of this kind of information can be found in *Meet the Authors* by Deborah Kovacs, and *Meet the Authors and Illustrators* by Deborah Kovacs and James Preller. *Something About the Author*, a set of reference books that some libraries have, contains information about children's book authors.

★ Discuss questions like these: *Why do you think people become authors? From where do you think authors get their story ideas? Which authors might you wish to contact? If you could ask them questions, what would you ask?*

★ Duplicate and distribute the brainstorm outliner on page 113. Students can use this organizer to jot down questions they might ask authors in a face-to-face discussion.

★ As an alternative, students might gather ideas they would want to ask people in other fields—a poet, a musician, a world leader, an athlete, or an astronaut. They can use the same brainstorm outliner by revising the categories.

★ GUIDE THE WAY

★ Remind students that authors need to work hard at their craft. They often struggle to rework ideas to get them just right. Guide students to ask realistic questions, keeping in mind that all writers have to think, plan, revise, and edit their work.

★ Students can also use the brainstorm outliner to freewrite about elements of the books that interest them. This may help them generate questions to ask.

Quality Questions—*Avoid asking simple* yes *or* no *questions. To get rich answers, ask thought-provoking questions, for instance: "What got you get interested in writing scary stories?", "What real-life people have you based any characters on?", "In what ways does [town] remind you of real places you have been to?", "How do you choose your characters' names?", "What is the hardest part of writing for you?", or "When did you begin writing?"*

★ FOLLOW IT UP

★ Have students draft letters to the authors and then mail them, in care of the publishers.

★ Have student authors hold discussions about stories they have written to share some of their own inspiration.

Name: _____

WRITE AWAY!
Ask An Author

 How do authors get their writing ideas? Ask them!
Think up good questions to get good answers.

Pick an author you like. Recall what you like about his or her work. Use the outliner below. Jot down ideas to help you ask some great questions.

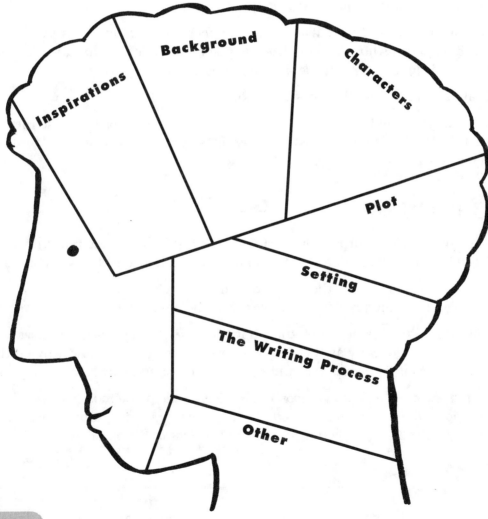

Inspirations

Background

Characters

Plot

Setting

The Writing Process

Other

And NOW—

Use your ideas to draft a letter to the author. Use your best ideas—ones that will inspire the author to respond. Include your return address so the author can find you.

Work Order

Students will write up work orders (repair memos) to describe something that needs fixing.

SET THE STAGE

★ Display pictures or brainstorm a list of things around the home, classroom, or work place that need to be fixed. Examples include a leaky faucet, a burned-out light bulb, a refrigerator that won't stay cold, a washing machine that overflows, a broken chair, a flat tire, a hole in a ceiling, and so on.

★ Collect and display examples of actual work orders or repair forms so students can see examples of this kind of practical writing.

★ Discuss questions like these: *What do you do when something needs fixing and nobody in your family knows how to do it? How do you think things get fixed in our school? Why would somebody write up a work order on paper?*

★ Duplicate and distribute the work order form on page 115.

★ Students might complete the work orders for real problems or for those they can imagine such as the lock on the classroom door gets stuck or the drinking fountain shoots out hot water. The problems can be realistic or humorous.

GUIDE THE WAY

★ Tell students that the purpose of a written work order (or service report) is to keep track of what goes wrong in a building and to record how effectively repairs are made.

★ Explain that in some cases, the work order must be clear enough so that a repair person can figure out the problem without anyone being there to explain what happened.

★ Point out that students need not know how to make the repairs themselves. But they should describe as clearly as they can what went wrong, when, and why—if they know. It helps to present the symptoms and point out the dangers or inconveniences.

> ***Stay on Track!***—*Exaggeration won't help. Even if the problem is big, or causes danger or disruption, stay direct. Provide facts. Describe what you did, saw, or heard, not how you felt. Give details that could help workers get right to the problem.*

FOLLOW IT UP

★ Discuss with students what kinds of information a repair person should write on the work order after the repair has been made.

★ Interview the janitor or office staff to find out how and when work orders are used around your school.

Name: _____

WRITE AWAY!
Work Order

🔑 A *work order* is a written request to fix something.
Work orders are used by companies, apartment buildings, or
other places where repair crews fix things for others.

✏️ Fill out the work order with all the key details. Describe what is broken and how it got
that way, or what doesn't work properly and how you know.

⭐ Name _____

⭐ Date _____

⭐ Location _____

⭐ Problem _____

_____

⭐ How It Happened _____

_____

_____

⭐ What You Think Needs to Be Done (optional) _____

_____

_____

⭐ Repaired by _____

⭐ Comments _____

_____

And NOW—

Write a letter to the repair crew. Explain more about the problem you outlined above. Tell why it is
inconvenient, unsafe, or troublesome. Tell why the repair should be done quickly. Even if you're
annoyed, take the time to be polite.

Parody

Students will write new lyrics for existing songs.

SET THE STAGE

★ Explain that *lyrics* are the words of a song. In many songs, the lyrics are like poems set to music.

★ Read the lyrics to favorite songs aloud as if they were poems. Emphasize meter, rhyme, rhythm, repetition, and how the lyrics fit the melody.

★ Tell students that a *parody* is an imitation of a serious work that pokes fun at the original. Parodies can be funny, silly, or serious. Most parodies are recognized immediately and make us laugh. They are great for enlivening parties and celebrations.

★ One parody that many students may know fits the tune of "Jingle Bells," and pokes fun at a famous cartoon superhero:

> *Jingle bells, Batman smells, Robin laid an egg*
> *Batmobile broke its wheels and the Joker got away!*

★ Discuss questions like these: *Have you ever made up funny lyrics to songs you know? What did you try to keep? What did you change? How can you tell if the new lyrics work?*

★ Duplicate and distribute the lyrics organizer on page 117.

★ Most parodies substitute new verses to existing songs. Musical learners may wish to write entirely new songs—melody *and* lyrics—in a spirit of fun.

GUIDE THE WAY

★ Point out the importance of meter. Lyrics won't work if there are too many words, or if the accented parts of words conflict with the accented parts of the melody.

★ Some students might fine-tune their lyrics by reciting them into a tape recorder.

★ The best way to test whether lyrics work is to try to sing them. If they are too hard to sing, then they need to be revised.

Word for Word—*Lyrics that work are easy to sing. They rhyme or move along smoothly. Try your lyrics a few times before you settle on them. Do the words work? Do they fit the melody? Do they rhyme where they should? Do they make a point? Will listeners recognize the original? Will they be amused?*

FOLLOW IT UP

★ Have a sing-off in which students share their lyrics in groups or for the whole class.

★ Make a tape of students' parodies. Compile a lyrics book for class sing-alongs.

Name: _____

★ WRITE AWAY!
Parody

 A *parody* is an imitation of a song that pokes fun at the original.

Pick a song whose words you know. Use your imagination and sense of humor to make a parody of the words.

The REAL Words	The Parody

And NOW—

Practice your parody. Sing it enough times to learn it by heart. Perform it for others.

More Ideas for Practical Writing

❏ Write notes to help you remember a news story.

❏ Write a thank-you note.

❏ Write a letter to your favorite grouch.

❏ Write a letter to an athlete who is having an off season.

❏ Write an answering machine message you might use in the school office.

❏ Write an answering machine message you might use at a doctor's office.

❏ Write a set of directions to leave for a baby-sitter.

❏ Write a description of where your family keeps first-aid supplies.

❏ Write a 911 script that involves a pet emergency.

❏ Write a job description.

❏ Write a letter asking for work.

❏ Write a letter asking how to open a bank account.

❏ Write a want ad to tell people about a tag sale or garage sale.

❏ Write a want ad to give away new kittens.

❏ Write to a librarian asking for help to research a topic.

❏ Write to a book illustrator about his or her artwork.

❏ Write a work order about a VCR that won't operate properly.

❏ Write a parody of a famous poem.

❏ Write a note to your teacher explaining why you were absent from school.

❏ Write to a game maker about changing the rules.

❏ Write to the local newspaper inviting them to cover the school science fair.

❏ Write a note to your family explaining why you went to the store.

❏ Write a set of directions for how to find the music store in the mall.

❏ Write a note to yourself reminding you about homework or about a test.

❏ Write a letter to the manager praising a worker at a store or restaurant.

The Big Book of Ready-to-Go Writing Lessons • Scholastic Professional Books

Reproducibles

Author's Award

is hereby presented to

_____

in recognition of
OUTSTANDING

_____

Teacher

Date

Name: _____

Editor's Marks

Begin a new paragraph here.

Make a capital letter.

Add a word here.

Take out a word or words.

Add a period.

Add a comma.

Add a quesion mark.

Check the spelling.

Does this sound right?

The Big Book of Ready-to-Go Writing Lessons • Scholastic Professional Books

12

Name: _____

Self-Evaluation Checklist

☐ Does your introduction grab readers?

☐ Is your purpose clear?

☐ Have you written for your intended audience?

☐ Have you get across your main ideas?

☐ Did you offer enough details, facts, or other information?

☐ Do your characters make sense? Do they speak and act as you want them to?

☐ Have you described the setting?

☐ Have you included sensory details?

☐ Have you cut out unnecessary details?

☐ Is your piece presented in sensible or logical order?

☐ Is your place presented in sensible or logical order?

☐ Have you used transition words?

☐ Does your conclusion work?

☐ Can you substitute vivid verbs, exciting adjectives, and other precise words?

☐ Have you used complete sentences?

☐ Have you used complete sentences? Do they end with the right punctuation?

☐ Do sentences begin with capital letters?

☐ you vary sentence style and length for interesting reading?

☐ Have you checked spelling and grammar?

Have you included a title?

The Big Book of Ready-to-Go Writing Lessons • Scholastic Professional Books

120

Certificate of Merit
for
Excellence in Writing
is presented to

_____

for

_____

Teacher

Date

⭐ Self-Evaluation Checklist

- ❑ Does your introduction grab readers?

- ❑ Is your purpose clear?

- ❑ Have you written for your intended audience?

- ❑ Did you get across your main idea?

- ❑ Do you offer enough details, facts, or other information?

- ❑ Do your characters make sense? Do they speak and act as you want them to?

- ❑ Have you described the setting?

- ❑ Have you included sensory details?

- ❑ Have you cut out unnecessary details?

- ❑ Is your piece presented in sensible or logical order?

- ❑ Have you used transition words?

- ❑ Does your conclusion work?

- ❑ Can you substitute vivid verbs, exciting adjectives, and other precise words?

- ❑ Have you used complete sentences?

- ❑ Do sentences begin with capital letters? Do they end with the right punctuation?

- ❑ Do you vary sentence style and length for interesting reading?

- ❑ Have you checked spelling and grammar?

- ❑ Have you included a title?

⭐ Editor's Marks

Begin a new paragraph here.   ¶

Make a capital letter.   the
                                                ‗

Add a word here.   first
                                               My ⌃dog

Take out a word or words.   on the o̶l̶d̶ front porch.

Add a period.   Ms⨀Klein

Add a comma.   red⌄yellow⌄green⌄and blue

Add a quesion mark.   Can you stay ⌄
                                                            ?

Check the spelling.   ⓢⓟ elepant

Does this sound right?   ⓚ? baby tooths

Certificate of Merit

for

Growth in Writing

is presented to

_____

for

_____

_____

Teacher

Date

Certificate of Merit

for

Excellence in Writing

is presented to

_____

for

_____

_____

_____ *Teacher*

_____ *Date*

Certificate of Merit

for

Originality in Writing

is presented to

for

_____

Teacher

_____

Date

Author's Award

is hereby presented to

in recognition of
OUTSTANDING

Teacher

Date

Notes

Notes

Notes